Heaven On The Hill

Shirley Romano

DEDICATION

God and my family who are the meaning of life itself.

ACKNOWLEDGMENTS

My daughter, Julie Ellis, for encouraging me to complete this book after it was initially completed fourteen years ago and for her patience in receiving each chapter in email then lovingly putting it all together. My granddaughter in law, Sarah Ellis, for sculpting the rough drafts into the beautiful story you find in your hands now.

CHAPTER 1

Mrs. Vivian Banks

We were finally off the main road headed to Winona, but it still seemed like forever riding in the dust.

"Honey, we're almost there," Morgan said again.

How many times had he said that?

Under her breath Cissy said, "Oh, to sit in a nice tub of water and get this dust and grime off me!"

The good doctor had talked of nothing else since he saw the ad in the newspaper about the land for sale in Mississippi. He loved his work but hated the day in and day out seeing patients from sunup to sundown with hardly ever a day off. He longed for the soil, the fields of wheat and horses grazing on his own land.

Turning to me, Morgan asked, "Viv, are we crazy for doing this?"

Cissy, sitting in the back, yelled out "Yes!" She was not the happiest young girl, moving all this way, leaving her friends, to come to an old dirt road leading nowhere it seemed.

Then Morgan pointed to a real nice house that sat back from the road on what looked like many acres of land. "Look, Viv, that's got to be the Judge's house. He's our closest neighbor."

"Is that good news or bad? It's sort of like living next door to the U.S. Marshall."

"And look there, Viv, Cissy. There our place is!" The house was very large and in rough shape from where we could see, still being way down on the road. It sat on a hill with trees all around and a couple out buildings scattered nearby. It was a pretty sight, but the closer they got the more run down the place looked.

"Daddy, how are we supposed to clean all that so we can sleep in it? It looks like no one has lived here for years."

"It will take some time, my darling daughter, but oh my you can get lost in the place, it has so many rooms. Fourteen, I think, and the coolest place in the day is on the lower level because it is partially underground."

"Where are we going to sleep tonight? Here?"

"Well, why not? We have our bedding in the back."

"What are we going to eat? Our box is almost empty."

"We will go into town or the nearest store to stock up on some food and oil for the lamps. We will just have to live out of our bags until we can get some more supplies."

"I don't see anything but land. No houses and no people."

"I know sweetheart, and that suits me just fine."

"Well, how are you going to see patients?"

"I'm not sure just yet. I may make house calls for a while."

"How are you going to find the people?"

"I'll manage, don't you worry your pretty little head about that, Cissy. By the way, this is what they call a plantation."

"I know and I feel like I'm in another country."

"It's quite different from what you're used to, but you will grow to love it."

"I hope you are right, but how can I love it if there are no people?"

"Give it time, Cissy, We'll find a church in town, and you'll see lots of people."

By this time I had already gotten in the house by the side door leading to the kitchen and found a huge sitting room with a fireplace.

When Morgan came in after me, I wrapped my arms around him and exclaimed, "Oh Morgan, I love it! Needs some major work, but we can do it."

Cissy ran on to the second level, skipping from room to room, saying "This one's mine, no, this one or maybe that one with all the windows across the back. Oh, my goodness! Daddy, may I please get a cat?"

"Oh honey, you won't have to get a cat, the cats will come to you. There are cats all over this place."

"Then may I have two?"

"Sure, honey."

"Daddy, are we going to have chickens?"

"Doggone right we are."

"What else, Daddy?"

"Well, let's get this place fenced in, and then see what we're going to put on the other side of it, ok?"

Being quiet all the way down here, Cissy was now suddenly full of questions and that's a good sign.

"Now Vivian, one of the first things we need to do is get some hired help and that might mean buying a couple slaves."

"Really?"

"That's what they do down here, Viv."

"Oh honey, buy a person?"

"I know, I hate the sound of that too, but that's all we can afford for the kind of help we need right now."

"Where will we keep them?"

"Right here in the house; we have plenty of rooms."

"What?"

"We have no other place, Viv. Would you have them sleep out in the yard?"

"Well, it's summertime."

"That wouldn't be the Christian thing to do."

"Won't they run away?"

"No, not when they find out we will treat them like human beings should be treated. Now, the first thing we need to do are make this house livable and build a shelter for the horses. Let's unload the wagon so we will have some room to bring back the things we need for the next few days. I'll take the horses down to the creek and cool them off." He led them down to the water for a drink and a bath. You can imagine how hard this trip has been on them.

Cissy and I took the things out of the wagon and stretched our legs. With Morgan back now, we three all sat on the porch. Morgan in an old rotted out piece of a chair, looked like he was in heaven, but I knew there was a lot on his mind concerning all that needed to be done and what to do next. My main concern was keeping Cissy safe with people I didn't know living in the house with us. It seemed not to worry Morgan or maybe he just didn't show it.

After about an hour and a half of resting, we were on the road again now with an empty wagon, looking for the store. There was only one, about four miles from our place. People watched us closely and the owner was somewhat friendly and somewhat not until he discovered instead of charging, Morgan was paying in cash Then he became real friendly. When Morgan told him we were the new folks in town who bought the old Hudson place, he said, "That's a pretty big spread, what do you plan to do with all that land?"

"A little of this and a little of that, but first I'm going to set up my practice and start seeing patients. I hear there is a big need for that around here?"

"You're right about that. There ain't no doctor for miles, both ways."

"Well, I aim to change all that."

"We've had doctors, we just can't keep 'em here. When you planning to start?"

"Just as soon as my supplies come in and I can find a couple rooms somewhere so I can have everything clean and set up."

"You won't have to wait long for business around here. You gonna deliver babies too?"

"Yes, I plan to. My wife is my assistant and she's good at it so between us that will be taken care of."

"Now, folks down in these parts don't have much and sometimes take a while to pay you."

"I understand that and am prepared to wait. I think we have everything we need and oh, some oil for the lamps. Alright, that ought to do it. Are the slaves sold tomorrow?"

"Yes, a little after one o'clock, on the block in front of the feed store. How many you fixin' to buy?"

"Don't know until I see them. Good day sir, be seeing you around."

"Good day to you too, and thanks for the business."

The road back was shorter or so it seemed. We road up around three o'clock and I found a basket left at our side porch with a note saying: "From your neighbors, Judge Catron and family. Welcome, so sorry we missed you."

"Well, how nice, Morgan. Go ahead and get yourself a plate if you can find one. There's enough for lunch and supper tonight, if we get hungry later on. I'll get it in where it's cool. So thoughtful of them to do that. What a spread!"

"Look, mama, fried chicken, potato salad, cornbread and sweet potato pie. Finally real food!" Cissy exclaimed as she dug in.

It was rough sleeping that night and they were sore the following morning. They ate the rest of the cornbread with strawberry jam for breakfast and wondered how long it would be before they had a comfortable bed to sleep in. Morgan was busy making a list of the things we would need for the slaves when they came to stay. There was one old bed left in a room on the third floor, so if we could get some kind of bedding one of us could sleep there. Thank goodness it was summertime, but we still needed wood for the cookstove which meant a saw for that. So many things to buy.

Cissy asked if the slaves would have any clothes. "I don't know," said Morgan, "If they don't, we will buy them some."

"How much are slaves, Daddy?"

"I really have no idea, Cissy, but I guess I'll find out this afternoon."

"Will you buy women slaves too, Daddy?"

"I don't know, I'll have to ask your mother how she feels about that."

On the way into town that day, Morgan asked me, "Vivian, if you are going to help me with the practice, don't you think we will need a of maid around the house for cooking and cleaning?"

"That depends on how fast your practice grows."

"The first few months might be slow."

"We need someone to stay with Cissy. She can't come with us every time we see a few patients. Maybe they will have some women slaves today too."

They spent a couple of hours at the supply store. Then Cissy and I wandered over to the mercantile store for fabrics and linens. About one o'clock, everyone gathered at the block for the sale. There were several people there and a few slaves lined up in chains. It made my heart sick to see it. There was no place to sit and I thought to myself, "this could take a while," so Cissy and I went into the store where it would be cool.

CHAPTER 2

Dr. Morgan Banks

Not long after the ladies went to cool off, the auction got started and the first man was bought quickly. Then I saw two young girls, who looked to be about eleven or twelve. The man said they were sisters. I heard the man say "sold" to Judge Catron, so I now knew what our neighbor looked like. I wandered over to say hello and to thank him for the basket of food. We didn't talk long as he wanted to get back home and I hadn't seen the people we needed yet.

Next up was a woman about forty years of age with a small child hanging onto her skirt. The man said they could be sold together or separate. Separate? Oh no! I began bidding and then another man bid, but just for the woman. I bid highest for both, and I had my first slaves. I had mixed feelings about the whole thing but couldn't let that child go without her mother.

Next up were two men looking to be sold together or separate. When I heard they were father and son, I began bidding with the rest of them. The man said because the father had runaway twice as a young man, he would sell them together as a "bargain" with the young one being the higher price since he would be a worker worth his money, so young and strong. I bid on both, having something in mind. Now with four instead of the three I came for I wondered

9

how we could all fit in the wagon but we did. When I looked around I said to myself, there were three of us and now there are seven.

No one talked on the way home, except me & Viv to each other, until we pulled up in front of the house.

Once everyone slowly got out of the wagon I said, "First, let's get these chains off you folks. This used to be the Hudson's place, but it's ours now. Don't know if you knew them or how they treated people, but let's go inside the house where it's cooler and we'll get to know each other better."

They looked at each other and came on in. We all sat in the sitting room, such as it was, minus a lot of furniture but cool, nonetheless. I introduced myself, "My name is Dr. Banks, this is my wife, Vivian, and my daughter, Cecilia. We bought most of this land as far as you can see on all four sides. Our first order of business in the morning is to fence in as much as we can and build a shelter for the horses. They will sleep up here close to the house tonight and hopefully it won't rain. First, I need to know your names." Pointing to the older man, "Your name?"

"They call me Ham, but my name is Abraham."

"And you son?"

"He be Jesse, Massa."

"Now one thing I want to say right now, no one call me master. We only have one Master and that's the good Lord. You will call me Dr. Banks, and Vivian here, you call her Mrs. Banks, and our daughter goes by many names. I call her "honey," "Cissy," or "Cecilia," but as you get to know her you will know what you wish to call her. Now, ma'am, your name?"

"Violet, sa."

"No, call me Dr. Banks, I prefer it."

"Yes sa, Dr. Banks."

"And your little one?'

"She be called Noël, 'cause she be born on Christmas day."

"Well now, how about that? Alright, the first thing we need to do is chop some wood for the cookstove, so we can eat tonight. Violet, I'm sure you and Mrs. Banks will come up with a good meal for everyone. What sort of things do you carry in your sack?"

"Mostly a change of clothes and things for my girl," said Violet.

The men left to cut wood and were back in an hour. Vivian had bought cabbages, meal, flour, eggs, fresh milk, beans, and a lot of potatoes and onions.

"I've never seen so many eggs. Cissy you and Noël take these eggs down to the cool room with the butter and milk."

"I have some cured sausages in my sack that a neighbor gave me this morning in town," said Ham.

"Thank you, Ham, for offering that. We will take that to the cool room as well and fry it for breakfast."

All the men including me sat on the porch and talked for a long time. I shared my plans for the house and the outbuildings. Maybe we could use one of the longest ones for the horses till we could build something better. Slowly Ham reached in his sack and pulled out his most treasured possessions, his tools. I was surprised he also pulled out a Bible, probably by mistake, and shoved it back in his sack.

Everyone was so hungry, that the smells from the kitchen were almost too much to bear. Finally, everyone was led to the kitchen to fill their plates and pick a barrel or a stool to sit on while two or three of the others just sat outside on the porch steps in the cool.

After dinner was cleaned up we all headed to bed. Cissy was a little frightened and slept on the floor next to me and Viv that night.

CHAPTER 3

Violet

When Dr. Banks was asking our names, we slaves looked at each other in a way that only we know, unbelief that we were not chained on the first day with our new master. How could that be? It didn't seem right and we waited to see if things would change as they usually do.

After dinner we were so puzzled about this new state of affairs because the two owners we had before this would rarely even speak to us unless it was an order. Heaven forbid that we ate together, that just wouldn't happen.

It was getting along toward dusk, and everyone was bone tired. When we looked at each other and wondered which tree we would sleep under, Dr. Banks said, "You all have had quite a day and everyone is tired, so pick yourself a room upstairs and see if you can get any sleep with the blankets you have. We will have better accommodations after we go into town again and bring back more provisions than people. Tomorrow we will have breakfast at half past seven and then get some work done in the cool of the morning." Ham led Jesse, me and Noël up the stairs with almost a look of fear. Our concern was this treatment was bound to stop any minute now. We talked among ourselves about this, and the fact that we weren't chained or confined in any way which meant we could have easily walked away this very night. Dr. Banks had even said grace with us before supper which was unheard of. He had even thanked the Lord for bringing us good people to him, when in fact he paid for us which didn't make no sense at all. Things were bound to be different tomorrow.

We were up early before anyone else that next morning. I had started a fire in the stove and the aroma of coffee filled the house. Dr. Banks and Cissy were next to get to the kitchen and Vivian slept a while longer. Dr. Banks mentioned that the trip had put a kink in her back and she felt lying there a little longer would be good for it.

Cissy and Noël ran to the cool room for the sausage, eggs, and a little milk for the biscuits. Everybody went ahead and ate without Vivian cause they needed to get started with their plans, saying grace once again, asking God to bless their day and keep them safe from harm.

Cissy watched over Noël taking her outside to play and reading her a story. I put breakfast in the warming side of the stove for Vivian, then found an old broom to start clearing away some webs and dust from the two rooms.

Vivian came into the kitchen thinking out loud as she ate breakfast, "If we only had a few chairs here and there, plus we need a table too. There are just too many things we need and I don't know what to do first."

I explained, "Ham can make furniture, at least a table and some chairs."

"Really, how did you know that?"

"I know 'bout him," is all I would say.

Early the next morning while there was a breeze, Ham and Jesse set out to cut wood. After breakfast, Viv, Cissy, Noël, and I went for a walk, way behind the house to see if they could find some blackberries. They picked enough for me to make a pie for supper and turned back to the shade of the trees in the yard.

While we were resting I turned to Mrs. Banks and explained, "Mrs. Banks, we getting a little short on things to fix. I hear, after church on Sunday, the white folks put out a spread in the church yard. You can buy beans, squash, corn, canned pork and jellies. They make a few pies and cakes to sell too. Half goes to the church and half yours."

"Well fine, I'll see what I can do there tomorrow. I want Morgan to fix me a chicken coop soon. I know he's got every minute filled with more important things, but sure would like some fresh eggs for breakfast. If you want to bake a pie or two, we'll try to sell them tomorrow and you can have your half of the money."

Violet couldn't believe what she was hearing. "Thanks, Mrs. Banks. If I make a blackberry pie, I won't need no eggs."

Ham, Jesse and I had been talking late at night about the situation. Jesse felt like things had got to change, cause nobody treated slaves like Morgan and Viv did. When word gets out they are like they are, there's got to be trouble. There are rules and laws about slaves.

CHAPTER 4

Dr. Banks

During the day, Ham, Jesse & I worked alongside each other putting up fencing until around one o'clock when everyone stopped for lunch. Ham had visited one of the sheds and found some boards that could work as a gate till they could do better. After lunch, we cleared away the junk in one of the larger sheds and fixed it to keep the horses in just in case it happened to rain. It was hard work and Ham removed his shirt when he got awful hot in the shed. I let out a cry in horror at seeing his back with the deep scars. It looked like he had been beaten and more than once. "How did you withstand that kind of pain, Ham?"

Ham said nothing, but I could not get that out of my mind the rest of the day. "How about your boy, has he been beaten too?"

"No sa, Dr. Banks, just worked to death from sunup to sundown and kept his mouth shut."

"How old is he?"

"He be 'bout fifteen now."

"He's a fine young man and I will promise you one thing, he will never be beaten here, never!"

"Thank you sa, I mean Dr. Banks. If you don't mind me asking, what kind of doctor you be? Can you sew people up?"

"Yes, Ham."

"Are you gonna be a doctor or a farmer, Dr. Banks?"

"I want to do a little of both. My father was a doctor and I, being his only child, was taught by him to be a doctor as well. It was mostly his desire that I follow in his footsteps, but I also love the land. When pop died, he left me with a longing to still come to the country and plant fields of corn, wheat, and vegetables. It's somehow born in me, but being a doctor has it's good points, too. I just want to do more than one thing in my life and my wife is good enough to follow me in my dreams and wishes. So here I am, just a mite older than you, and it will be a job getting this whole thing started."

"I be tellin' you, Dr. Banks, you the first white man that's sat down and talked to me like I was more than a hog, or a cow. If word gets around, other white folks won't stand for it."

"Now just what do you think they do about it? How I treat the people who work for me is nobody's business but mine. I suggest you and your boy just not to mention it to anyone. If they ask you, just say he's a good boss, that's all."

"Yes, sa, Dr. Banks, 'cause word travels fast when some slaves got it better than others. Most overseers don't much like it. Some been known to take it out on 'em. My boy asked me why you be different, lettin' us sleep in your house and such."

"I'll answer those questions later, but for now you give me a good day's work and I'll give you a good days' pay, the same food I eat, and a place to stay out of the weather. Now I suggest in your spare time you start carving out a bed for you and Jesse. I was told you have a carpenter's touch with things like that. We're gonna cut some of those bigger trees on the other side of the hill and you can use some of that wood. Summer will be gone before you know it, and you need a warm bed for a good night sleep."

"Yes, sa, Dr. Banks, I can do that, but what 'bout the women folk?"

"It's more important for now that you get a bed because you're working harder and if you can do that, then maybe a table for us to eat on. Could you and Jesse sleep together for a while?"

"Yes sa."

"Then do that for a while."

"But see if you goin to keep us in your house at night, people won't agree on that."

"Well, like I said, whose going to know if you don't tell? Keep your thoughts to yourself, we have more than enough room here for you."

Later that evening the seven of us sat around after supper and I asked Ham to pull out his Bible. Ham didn't know I had seen it that first day. When Ham sat back down with his Bible, I asked Ham if he would like to read the Bible to us. He said, "No sa, I just know a few words, like Jesus, Lord, and God." So I asked if he would like for me to read a little from it. "Oh yes sa, nobody read it for a good while."

So, I read several verses and when I was through, Ham reached for his harmonica and played, Shall We Gather At the River. The sound of the music out in the open was enough to put you to sleep. Little Noël's eyes were just about closed, so Violet took her on up to the room and tucked her in.

HEAVEN ON THE HILL

Then she and Cissy washed the dishes as Ham and Jesse got some wood for the cookstove in the morning. Ham, Jesse and I sat on the porch and planned for the next week what the most important things there were to be done.

In the morning, our family would ride into church. The church was real close to town, but far enough out for people to park their buggies and wagons. There were about forty people that came that day. There was no piano and just an old man with a beat-up guitar to make the music for the hymns. The preacher was neither good nor bad so the music for the most part was the most pleasant thing that Sunday.

Afterwards we got to meet some of the folks and Judge Catron was there with his two sons. They said, his wife was sickly and rarely attended. There were several children Cissy's age and we asked about school. We were told there were about fourteen or fifteen in all that attended from ages seven through fifteen. Most of them went from five to eight years because they were needed too badly for chores and harvesting. The teacher doubled as the Sunday school teacher as well. She was about as pretty as they come and some said that was the reason they had as many as they did for church and school.

CHAPTER 5

Vivian

After church, just as Violet had said, a long table was set up outside for the food to buy. A woman at the end of the table sat to take the money, with half going to the church and the other half to the seller. Violet had made two blackberry pies and they were bought so quickly that I thought I couldn't find them, but that was because they were bought up so quickly. There were tomatoes galore, fresh shelled green peas, corn, and jars of just about everything you could think of. We grabbed up the last jar of canned pork and were ready to go home, hoping each week we could do this through the winter. In the spring we would buy a couple hogs, a cow or two, another horse for plowing, and maybe another slave to help in the fields. Our family was doing so well with who we had, we hated to try someone new for fear they may not get along so well together. Morgan would just have to pray about that.

We needed to get started with some chickens, so we started a small henhouse in the backyard not too far from the house to make getting eggs easier and to keep the chickens safer. They won't produce that many eggs during the winter months, but even an egg for each person a day and a couple for baking would keep us from having to buy so many at church.

Morgan had been called out several times for minor illnesses and a fracture or two. Only one family had paid him, giving him a country ham, till they could raise the money. He looked at each situation and decided if that would be enough payment. Our family could eat on that ham for a week or more. Most of the folks were desperately poor and if that was the case, he didn't charge them at all.

When the white folks told the council that he had treated one of the slaves' children, they talked among themselves for days. They felt he had stepped over the line when he wasn't called in by the slave owner and proceeded to do as he pleased. The next day two men came riding out to the house and asked for Morgan. I told them he was out working on the place, so, they rode out and found him hammering away at a shelter.

Morgan told me later they greeted each other and stated their business. He told them he was here to treat any person who called him, black or white, and that they all needed a doctor, so he would treat the slaves as well. The men said, "We don't do things that way around here."

Morgan's response to that was, "maybe that's why no doctor would stay here but a few months. Now if you all want to set your own broken bones, deliver your own babies, complicated or simple, catch the cholera in time or any other health problems, just let me know. In the meantime, let me be the judge of who I treat." The men said nothing but left in a huff.

During the week to come Judge Catron called on Morgan twice, the first being a case of pneumonia in one of his sons and the second call came late one night for one of his slaves; a young girl who was bleeding badly. When Morgan examined this girl, a mere child of about twelve, he told the Judge, "Someone has messed with this child in a dishonorable way and whoever did this should be horse whipped or worse. I really need to take her home and keep an eye on her." The Judge wouldn't allow it, so he left medicine and asked for her to have bed rest for a week, no less. Morgan told the Judge if he was ever called to the place again, he would find out what kind of problems the Judge had with his slaves or anyone else that was handling the child in this manner. The Judge sort of pushed him out the door and thanked him more than once for coming out in the middle of the night.

When Morgan got home, he told me the entire way back that he couldn't get out of his mind that something was going on in that house and he must keep a close watch. He was not called back to check on the child, so we all prayed she had healed. We had an idea that one of the sons was responsible for this and the more Morgan thought about it, the angrier he got crying out, "Lord, please help this young girl."

CHAPTER 5

Dr. Banks

When me and Ham went into town the next day, we got all kinds of stares. Word had gotten around now about how we treated our slaves. Ham was feeling a little uncomfortable about now and I told him they wouldn't do anything with his owner with him. Ham was afraid to be left in the wagon while I talked with the person in charge of renting him some property so I told him, "I will keep my eyes on you while I'm inside and remember there is always the gun under the seat for your protection as well as mine.

Mr. McBroom talked about several places available, but then he brought up the fact that I was doctoring the slaves. To which I responded, "What of it? They get sick just like you and I."

"We don't treat our slaves that way. Maybe they don't do that way up north where you're from, but they stay in their place here and when they get sick, they doctor themselves."

"And if they don't get well?"

"Then we let 'em die, they're only slaves. They don't even have any money to pay you."

"Well, there are town folk who don't pay either."

"I don't want to rent you rooms here and have a bunch of darkies lined up in the street to see you."

"I wouldn't let them stand outside waiting."

"I'll have to bring this matter up before the town council and let them decide."

"May I speak for myself at the meeting?"

"I'm not sure about that just now."

There were slaves on the block that day, but I didn't plan to buy one. Several people watched while Ham came and went as he pleased, just as if he belonged to no one. They were very skeptical of me. We got the rest of our supplies and left in the wagon, talking about the problem all the way home.

On my next visit to a house a few miles away, one afternoon, I took Jesse with me. "I need your help on this one, Jesse, and if they don't accept you, don't say a word; I'll handle it." The man, who rode out to get him this morning, said it was a bullet in man's arm.

Vivian normally would go with me on a case like this, but she and Violet were right in the middle of canning some of the fresh green beans they got from church. Besides Jesse had asked questions and seemed interested in my work, so I decided to take him. When we came up to the porch after arriving, the father came to the door and said, "Come in, but leave him outside."

I went in and saw that the son of the man had a nasty wound. We would have to remove the bullet. "I will need my helper to assist me so please allow him to come in."

"I don't want no slaves in my house."

"Well then, we will just operate in the yard here if you can bring something for him to lie on."

"In the yard?"

"Yes, I won't be able to do this alone."

"Can't I help you?"

"Well sir, most of the people who have tried can't stand to even watch and most faint dead away in a couple minutes."

"Alright then, bring him on in but just here in the kitchen, nowhere else."

"Ok, clean away your table here and I need a couple pots of boiling water." I motioned for Jesse to come in and he stood beside me after scrubbing real good. Jesse held the instruments while I held the wound open and probed around for the bullet. I looked at Jesse and he was as calm as could be doing everything he was told to do without apprehension. After removing the bullet and waiting till the son awakened, we went into the next room and the father told Jesse to go outside. I showed the man how to dress the wound and keep it clean instructing him if he saw any infection, to come and get m.

The man said, "How much do I owe you?"

"Whatever you can give."

As they rode away on horseback, the father looked as puzzled as could be and not too happy about the situation. He decided he wouldn't tell anyone that he allowed that darkie in his house; it just might cause him trouble. Jesse seemed happy that I was so pleased with his help. I told Jesse, "You got a steady hand and a strong stomach. That's what it takes, among other things. We may just be on to something here."

CHAPTER 6

Jesse

The women spent most of the summer sewing blankets and canning as much food as they could for the winter months ahead. Pa built a bed and is working on a big kitchen table which was almost ready. I cleaned out the chimney in the big fireplace in the sitting room to get it all ready for winter. Dr. Banks told me that since the room is large enough that if we had to keep warm in the bitter weather, all of us could gather in there and sleep by the fire. The women cooked some of the best meals anyone had ever had. Summer corn was in and the church on Sunday had piles of it for sale.

Dr. Banks sat with me in the late evenings to teach me as much as he could without the me having any schooling. We would really have a time if anyone knew that Cissy was teaching me how to read and write. You could be whipped or hung for that and Dr. Banks stressed the fact. "When you are around white or black folks, don't let on you can do any of that. This is our family secret."

I missed my friends, even though things were horrible at the place before I came here. I would come in each night so sore I couldn't stand to eat and went straight to bed to get ready for the next day's labor. I'll never forget how bad I was treated; even the old coon dogs got a pat on the head now and then.

Speaking of dogs, Dr. Banks bought two beagle pups from the store on the road. There was a litter in a box by the stove in the back. They were ready to give away, so Dr. Banks picked one and Pa picked the other. On the way home they decided to name one Rock and the other one Rowdy. They were barkers all right and let everyone know if anyone was out there around the place. Cissy was a little upset as she had asked for a cat and Morgan said, "Soon, Cissy. I know it won't be long before those cats smell the good food cooking and especially the fish Ham and Jesse have caught. They'll be coming around soon; I just know it."

The outbuildings were taking shape and Pa was helping Dr. Banks work on the henhouse, cutting out little holes for each hen. Dr. Banks said they would buy little chicks soon so they would be a pretty good size by fall which got me thinking.

CHAPTER 7

Dr. Banks

By this time, I had received my second shipment of medicine, bandages, etc., which meant I was ready to get my practice going, but I still hadn't heard from the real estate man. I decided it was time to go back to town and see what council had said. Mr. McBroom met with me again and said council had voted he could not rent me a space if I saw slaves as patients. "Your town will lose a lot of revenue if I don't practice in town and the distance for me to ride to see you when you need me will cause a lot of deaths if I can't reach you in time. I might have to make a decision on my vocation and just be a full-time farmer at this point." Mr. McBroom raised his brow and his face flushed with worry as everyone knew I had the money to do just that. Since the Judge was my neighbor & I had helped him several times already I asked, "What did the Judge say about this?"

"Well, he knows you have already delivered three difficult births which would have otherwise resulted in death for the baby and probably the mother as well. But slaves are slaves and he doesn't want them lined up in town waiting to see you either. We just don't do this sort of thing here in our town."

"Well Mr. McBroom if your wife or daughter or any member of your family had to make a choice as to have me come save one of your precious family members, what would you do?" To which I received no response, so I walked away and rode back home with a feeling of defeat, but I was not done yet.

Two days later a council member rode out to our place and ran right inside the door of our kitchen where everyone was seated for our noonday meal. "Please come Dr. Banks, my daughter's first child is coming, and it's been fourteen hours of labor already. I fear she and her baby will die if you don't come right away. Please Dr. Banks."

"Alright, Jesse come with me." We rode out to the house and entered the room where the daughter lay in a pool of blood and sweat. She was very young, and I could tell right away that the baby was in breach position.

I ordered everyone out of the room. The people gasped as Jesse sat close-by while I pushed and turned the baby. Then in a couple minutes I delivered the child. The mother lay exhausted but all right. We then turned to leave the house without saying a word.

That family too would never mention how a young negro slave came in this house and helped deliver a healthy baby who would otherwise have died along with its mother. I never asked for a nickel for my services. Two weeks later the man and his wife rode out to our home and left so much food, beef, and money but no note of thanks.

That night Ham, Jesse and I sat talking well into the night. Ham said he was scared cause that man is on the council and if anyone heard about this, the councilman would have to vacate his seat which meant he would lose his good paying job. I responded, "When the problems seem unsolvable, turn them over to the Lord and He will work it out." So, we prayed and asked God to work this problem out. This was the way we always handled our problems.

I continued to work the farm including buying the chicks and putting them in one of the rooms with a fireplace to keep them warm until they could regulate their own body temperature. We put down papers from an old medical journal and then boards all around so the baby chickens couldn't get out. Cissy and Noël took care of them and suffered when two or three died, but they loved those little darlings. When time came for them to be put in the henhouse, they called it graduating to a higher class. They checked on them every day so nothing would harm them. Rock and Rowdy kept watch in case an undesirable animal approached. Those dogs were well worth their price when it came to keeping watch over the property.

CHAPTER 8

Cissy

One early morning in late August, Mommy came to my room and said, "Get up sweetheart, you have a visitor."

"What?"

"Someone's here to see you."

"This early, who in the world?"

Still in my nightgown, I went down to the lower level and Mommy said, "They are on the porch there."

"They?"

"Yes, open the door."

So, I opened the door. At first, I didn't see anything at all and then I saw a huge black cat over in the corner of behind the wood box. "Oh, my goodness!" I exclaimed. Slowly one after another three little ones appeared: one grey, one black like its mother and one was white with black spots. "Oh mommy, they are here!"

"Your Daddy said they would be if you'd just wait a bit. You asked for two and got four. Oh, they are beautiful, and you know what? By spring they will be old enough to stay in the barn and catch the mice."

"Can they stay up close to the house while they're little?"

"Sure, and their mamma cat will take care of them a good while longer. Just like your Daddy said they would smell the fish frying and they surely did. Or I should say their mamma did and knew where to bring her family to be fed."

So Noël and I did more mothering of this special family than the mamma cat did. The kittens put on a show for us on a regular basis. I've never been so happy. I tended to Noël most of the time and that freed Violet up to help Mommy in the kitchen.

Daddy and Ham set out for town to get us some piglets. Jesse knew exactly how to care for them and keep them warm as the fall season began.

I started school but since it was harvest time, only went three days a week. Daddy and Ham would drive me in on those days, carrying a loaded shot gun with them as we never knew what people might do.

The people still called on Daddy but did it on a real private basis, not letting anyone know they had called him to their home. First the measles or a snake bite or the croup or any number of other illnesses and an occasional birthing of a baby, but no one said a word about him opening his practice in town. The women were more prone to get him to come and seemed to dare their husbands to say a word.

On Sunday while singing the hymns, people began to notice that Mommy had a lovely voice and listened while she out sang everyone else reaching the high notes so beautifully. On one song everyone else stopped singing just to hear her voice. They found that more and more people were attending since she began singing. A piano would have made her sound even more beautiful. She was asked many times to sing a solo on Sundays and she didn't mind at all. Even though she was shy, she had confidence in her voice, and it showed.

CHAPTER 9

Dr. Banks

One of the council members daughters was getting married and they asked Vivian if she would sing at her wedding. Vivian said, "I will, if you will allow me to have Ham play for me on his harmonica." Well, she had asked him something there. The father would have to think about it, but not the mother as she had already told Vivian that she and her daughter wanted nothing more than have Vivian sing.

When the man approached the council about the matter, the lead councilman said, "You Banks family again, trying to bring your slaves in on everything." They voted and it was a tie, five to five.

The father approached the council again and said, "Now listen, I know how everyone feels about having a negro come into our church but this is not like Sunday service. He will only come in to play for Mrs. Banks and then leave. That's it, that's all. Now the woman needs music to make it all sound right so please vote again, if I persuaded one of you to make it six to four."

So, they cast their concealed votes again, and no one knew of course who changed his mind this time but it was six to four in favor of having music. This was a first in a white church, having a Black person enter, except while building the church of course.

Ham looked so handsome, dressed in one of my suits and he played beautifully for Vivian, who made the wedding a success. She sang two songs and looked lovely, but Ham sat out the rest of the festivities in the wagon out the back of the church. Not one person came up to him after the wedding to complement or thank him but he didn't seem to mind as he told me later just the thought of what had just happened made him proud. Later, of course, Vivian thanked Ham and told him what a terrific job he had done.

Ham, Jesse and I sat up late talking about what the next order of business should be as far as the outbuildings. The one large shelter had been extended upward including had a better roof with solid door to keep out the wind and rain, but it was so small that it could only hold our two horses, Barney and George. A new outbuilding would have to wait until spring when we get a few cows and maybe another horse. We were considering the land and what needed to be planted. A place up closer to the house would do better for our vegetable garden so the women could help work it in their spare time.

The more Ham and I talked the more he opened up to me with conversation about the council and Judge Catron. And for some reason, the Judge was responsible for the other doctors leaving town. None of them lasted even six months. Ham said, there was a dark side to him and that he be messing with young slave girls. "If you watch Judge Catron, he always buys the young ones on the block at auction time and runs with them real quick, thinking no one be seeing what he's doing. He and his overseer are terrible to their slaves, making them work long hours, punished for things you wouldn't think bad at all. They are given practically no money and the food is left over or picked over. He threatens them and whips them on a regular basis. If they argue among themselves, they not only get whipped but separated from their wife and children. All his buddies on the council are pretty much like him and they want you to be like them. They thought you were just a farmer coming down here, not a doctor."

"Ham, when was the last time they had a doctor down here?"

"Oh, been 'bout a year, I'd say."

"And you all have never been treated by any of them?"

"No, we just used our old fashion remedies we been usin' down through the years and we lost some good folks doin' it too."

"Now how about the Judge's sons, are they pretty good boys?"

"Ones pretty wild like and the other one is no trouble so I hear, but that Judge loves his boys."

"What's his wife sick with?"

"Don't rightly know Dr. Banks, they just say she be sickly. Don't think anybody knows for sure 'bout that. Dr. Banks, nobody treats slaves good like you do so how come you be different? If folks really knew how you treated us, they would come after you."

"Well Ham, I believe the Bible is an instructional book on how we are to live and treat others. All through the Bible it says love and forgive. The trouble is most people only believe in parts of it and the other half don't even read it. They come to church to look good and soon as they leave, they continue in their old ways. I believe if you treat people fairly, they will treat you the same which goes for your family and help, too. I believe in prayer for my needs and problems. If He knows every hair on our heads, He knows how things need to be worked out. If we love Him and obey his commandments, he will never let us down. That don't mean we won't suffer and have problems, but He will see us through all of that. Ham, how come you ran away and got those beatings?"

"I feared my children were being mistreated and I wanted to go get 'em."

"You have other children?"

"Yes, two girls and I know where they are now but scared to say."

"Ok, that's all right, in your own good time you can tell me. In the meantime, we will gather after supper and pray about this." Ham had tears in his eyes which I had never seen before in this more than six foot strongly built man, but I had seen the sadness there before.

CHAPTER 10

Vivian

The days were getting shorter, meaning less time to work and normally we would be harvesting, but we had nothing to harvest. I'm sure the winters here will in no way be like the ones we had up north. Still, we have to make sure we have plenty of feed for the horses and chickens; the pigs can live off our scraps from the kitchen. We will have to make sure our cabinets are full. Violet and the girls have done a good job canning everything from the church vegetables. Jesse will keep us with wood for the cookstove and for the fire in the sitting room fireplace. We need oil for the lamps, gunpowder for if and when someone finds out our slaves are living in our house with us. Ham had made several chairs while I had sewn pillows to make the seats more comfortable and warmer. We are pretty well set for any kind of weather.

Cissy has gotten several books from the Sunday school at church, and she wants a tablet to write on so she can teach Noël everything she learns in school. She's also taught Jesse a little about numbers, so he can measure things better. Jesse hasn't had time to learn to write his name yet, but he certainly will this winter.

Morgan, Violet, and I will go into town today to buy more yarn, material, etc. to make warm clothes and sweaters. It's amazing how

Violet and I can sew and knit everything we need. The fishing is still good which the cats love, so we try to eat as much of that while we have plenty and save the canned goods for the time when we need it most.

But this horrible feeling that we must hide from everyone is really uncomfortable. Violet says you either have to conform to their ways or hide a lot and pray they don't find out about much.

That evening, like every evening we all sat in front of the huge stone fireplace in the sitting room, and Morgan read from the Bible Afterwards every man, woman and child would get down on their knees in front of our chairs. Morgan would lead us in prayer and sometimes each person would pray for his or her needs. It truly was the best part of the day, and everyone went to bed feeling that God would take care of them just like He said He would.

The trees were almost bare now and dark came early. Even still Morgan insisted we all have a job to do including lessons, wood working, music and reading. He believed in growing and using your talents and time to the fullest.

Morgan was still called out sometimes in the night. The people would ride up to the house which caused Rock and Rowdy to bark ferociously warning us someone was approaching. They banged on the door until Morgan would come. Then he would get dressed in a hurry and be out of there as soon as he saddled up "old George," who was not really all that old but he still called him that. He got his lantern and his doctor's bag then off he went, letting the caller lead the way. He insisted they lead him back if it was the first time somewhere.

On this night it was a birthing and to Morgan's surprise, twins this time. He was paid in goods and promised to pay more come spring. They had not lost a single baby since Morgan had been here, but not everyone knew he was still practicing medicine. They kept it quiet, but they felt secure in the fact that if they needed him, he would come and who wants to lose a child or the mother? Morgan was told that last year they lost four babies and one mother because of complications. They couldn't afford to lose him so they kept it from the other council members and asked Morgan not to mention that he had delivered their children.

A week or two before Thanksgiving every year the town had a barn dance, called the Harvest Dance. Everyone for miles around came bringing pies and cakes, which were the favorites, along with every other thing imaginable. It was always the best time of the year, that, and Christmas.

The slaves came too and had a big bonfire a few yards away. It was the only time the slave owners allowed them to pretty much be on their own, except for a couple of men who took turns to see that no one slipped away. Most of them rode in on the back of their owner's wagon.

Cissy, who would turn fourteen in a few months, was having the time of her life, square dancing with someone different each dance. She had blue eyes, like me with long black hair and beautiful skin. I know I am partial, but she really was by far the loveliest girl there. Everyone knew it too including Morgan, so he kept a close watch on her. Judge Catron's son, Jeff, also kept a close eye on Cissy. He was very popular with the girls and was already sixteen.

"He was so nice," Cissy said on the way home, so gentle and proper, nothing like his brother who was known to have a temper like his dad starting fist fights at the slightest provocation. Jeff's brother wasn't nearly as handsome as his brother either. I guess it was hard being the Judge's son; just like being a preacher's kid.

Anyway, fun was had by all, and they rounded the bend to their house around eleven-thirty with Ham, Violet, and Jesse riding in the back of the wagon with Cissy and Noël.

The next day, Jessie and Ham told Morgan there was talk last night about the way we treat our slaves like they are family. Some were just plain jealous, others wondered how they came by such luck, but if word gets to Judge Catron, we will be in for it. So, we best be careful day and night. Some asked where they are sleeping now that nights were colder? Jesse said, "I just told 'em we had our own place and that really wasn't no lie. I just didn't tell 'em it was in our master's house."

CHAPTER 11

Dr. Banks

Mississippi had a colder winter than usual, and it started around the first of December. Violet and Vivian had sewn blankets for the horses specially to use after I had to go out in the night. I carried a couple for old George if he had to stand and wait very long in the rain or snow for me. There was a lot of pneumonia and earaches with the elderly suffering more than most.

On a stormy night in early December, Judge Catron had one of his sons ride out for me and that was hardly what I expected to ever happen, but it certainly did.

This call was for his wife and when I arrived, I saw that the woman was in a state. Mrs. Catron was shaking, yelling, and pulling her hair out. She wouldn't let anyone come near her, not even her maid, who had been with her for twenty years. I ordered everyone into the next room while I examined her. It was obvious she had some kind of trauma on this day, but she wouldn't reveal the nature of it. I explained to her if she didn't calm down, I would have to restrain her and she wouldn't want that.

"You don't have to tell me anything you don't want to tonight Mrs. Catron, but when you're ready to talk, I'll be glad to listen."

I went out and told the others that she should sleep now for the night but to try not agitating her in any way. If she was worse tomorrow, please come and get me, but if she was resting, let her.

"She had something really upset her, does anyone here know what that might be?" No one spoke.

For several days I didn't hear anything from them, but last night Judge Catron came up to the house. Of course, everyone hid except Violet and Noël. He insisted on paying me a lot of money which I said I couldn't accept. But the Judge made me take it anyway and then added, "Please don't say anything about this to anyone as this sort of outburst was not like my wife." It was almost like him paying me off to keep me quiet which is how I took it.

The nights would have been long, but we made each day and every night pleasant. After the chores and chopping the wood for the next day or two, this day even more as we felt snow was coming in the air. You know how that is and we felt it all day. We ate a good meal of turkey that Jesse had killed with corn fritters and cabbage. Then we topped it off with a mile high applesauce cake with a topping that Violet made so delicious it made you feel you had died and gone to heaven. We all decided to sleep in the sitting room that night instead of going to our cold rooms. Several of the rooms had fireplaces but carting the wood up and keeping watch on it all night felt like too much work. So, we decided to lie up close to the fireplace on the main level with our bedrolls talking, singing, and praying well into the night.

I noticed through the window just before I went to bed that it had already begun to snow while we were all cozy, warm and at peace. Just as I was drifting off to sleep, Rock and Rowdy began to bark and really cause a ruckus out there in the snow-covered yard. When they did that, they usually meant business, so I jumped out of bed, got my gun, took one down for Ham and we ventured out into the cold night.

The dogs stayed close beside us till they got close to the pig pen and started pulling away just as they came upon the pigs squealing in their pen.

"What is going on out here?" I asked.

The dogs kept barking and the pigs were huddled to one side out from under the roof of the pen, getting covered with snow. When I came closer and shined my lantern into the shed, I saw a young slave girl hiding in the corner.

"What in the world are you doing out here in the cold and in this pen?"

She was shivering so I wrapped my coat around her and carried her until we got to the house. When we came into the kitchen door, I put her down and removed my coat from around. Then Violet and Ham ran to the girl throwing their arms around her while crying her name. "Lizzy, Lizzy! Oh, my darlin, my precious child, you've come to us. How did you find us?"

The child was so distraught, it was hard to get any questions answered right then. We eased her into the sitting room by the fire. Then covered her nearly frozen feet as she had to flee into the night in a hurry and couldn't find her shoes. We feared she had frostbite, depending on how long she had been outdoors. The puzzled look on Vivian and my face was a mix of alarm and questions. Then Jesse came to her and knelt beside her covering her with his blanket.

Jesse begged, "Lizzy, where have you been, we've missed you so, and where is Esther? Please tell us what is going on."

Vivian & I looked at each other and asked, "It's obvious you know this young girl."

Ham and Violet finally tore their eyes away from Lizzy and looked at us saying, "We were afraid to tell anyone about our situation, but

44

now that we know you to be a good and God-fearing family, we will tell you. She is our child just as is Jesse and Noël be our last child." We stood with our mouths open for what seemed like five minutes. Then we all hugged each other asking, "This is the one you prayed over each and every night?"

"Yes, and her sister."

"So there are four children?"

"Yes, and we have been together for eighteen years, but separated from our daughters Lizzy and Esther since about four years ago. The man who had us first didn't need many women and girls, so he split us up. Later when he sold his place along with most every slave he had, he sold Ham and Jesse. We knew we would never all be together again. The day you bought us was just pure luck, we happened to be what you needed at the time, but our girls went on the block before us. We never saw them or who bought them. When we came out, they had already left with their new master."

I was putting all this together in my mind about that day in July when I was first in town at the slave block. I had seen Judge Catron buy two young girls and whisked them away in his carriage as soon as he paid for them, but I just couldn't remember if it was the same girl.

So, I asked the young girl where she came from tonight. She was still trembling, but her Ham said, "It's ok Lizzy, this here is Dr. Banks and he is a good man. He has not and will not harm any of us. If you don't want to tell him, you can tell us later."

Morgan agreed with Ham. Violet who was still holding Lizzy when she fell asleep after having a hot bowl of stew from dinner, was truly happy. Everyone was so exhausted we went to sleep and were late getting to our chores the next morning. Thank goodness we didn't have any cows to milk yet, but the pigs were squealing, and Barney and George were more than ready to be let out and fed. The horses didn't stay out long because it had snowed about a half a foot, and they really had rather stay in their shelter eating hay.

Violet and Ham were so happy to be with their little girl once more. Since it would be snowing for a while and too hard to get to school, Cissy took Lizzy under her wing. They played together with the cats and Cissy showed her how to crochet. Lizzy opened up once she knew she was safe, a feeling she explained that she had never had before. Violet told Vivian that Lizzy had shared more about what had happened since they were parted, but she was too afraid to talk about what was happening at Judge Catron's house for fear Ham would do something terrible to the Judge and be hung in a tree for it.

CHAPTER 12

Vivian

Morgan, Ham, Violet, and I got together and decided to hide the child for fear someone would ask questions. They told Lizzy that since she was a runaway slave, the owner would be out searching for her, so we needed to keep her in the house for a while. Violet asked, "How long is a while?"

"Until we find out the truth about who she belongs to, then we will go from there."

So, for a good while they kept her out of sight and if anyone came up to the house, they would put her in the cellar, or cool room, where there was a door hidden by an old dresser that was left there before we bought the place. She knew she was not to move until some family member said the coast was clear.

I was the first to notice that the girl had a slight stomach which was very pronounced as she was a slim and frail little girl. When I told Morgan, he said, "Yes, she almost looks like she is with child." So, he went to Violet to ask her if she had noticed, and she said yes, but thought since she came here, she had eaten so much better that she was just getting a little chubby.

Morgan said, "But, Violet, she's only chubby around her middle. Every other part of her is as slim as before."

"Oh, Dr. Banks, you don't suppose she gonna have a baby do ya?"

"Well it's highly possible if she has already started her monthlies."

"I'll talk with her tonight. Oh, Dr. Banks, she just a child."

"I know Violet, but how old is she really?"

"She be 'bout twelve and a half."

"Well, our Cissy started her monthlies at eleven, so it's possible."

I could hardly sleep that night. Morgan and I began to worry about how we would conceal this child along with her pregnancy. It wasn't going to be easy.

Morgan told me what Ham had told him about the slave block and the two young girls who had been bought up by someone before they were even stood up on the block. He told me that he was sure Judge Catron had bought those two children and knows now they were sisters, Ham and Violet's daughters.

"The fact that the overseer or the slave owner will bed these girls does happen all the time Vivian."

"But that young?"

"They don't care, the younger the better for some perverted creatures. Now I feel I'm right about what's happened but not so sure who's doing the dirty work. Most likely his sons or his overseer but it could be, heaven forbid, the Judge. If he knew we had her or that I was on to him, we would be run out of town really quick, just like I think, the other doctors were gotten rid of. Well, I'm going to give him a run for his money. I think he will probably get someone to go snooping around here to see what or who he can find. We need to be extra careful about who comes on our land and for what reason. Don't let anyone in the house, just tell them to wait outside. Then you go outside and ask them to state their business. If it doesn't sound right, tell them to wait till you talk to me. You know how sometimes we have people just come by and want to look at the house; tell them it's not convenient today or whenever. Violet will let us know soon enough if our suspicions are true about Lizzy and then we will have to make a few plans to cover this thing up for a while."

"How long is a while?"

"Well, you know sometimes girls these young have a struggle and may lose the baby. We will just have to wait and see."

"How far along do you think she is?"

"I would venture to guess about three to four months; that is without examining her."

"That far? Oh my."

Ham and Violet were both happy and afraid. It was hard to keep their minds on their work with the arrival of this little girl. Ham asked, "Please Dr. Banks, help us keep our child."

"I'll do my best to see that she is not taken away, but you know by law, she belongs to him and if she is found, may have to be taken back. But Ham when our problems and fears are too great to handle, we must take it to the Lord. He says fear not and to cast your troubles on Him. To tell you the truth, I don't think it was an accident that you and your family were to come to us that day. I believe God was in control of the error that was made that day and sent a good part of your family to us. And now your little Lizzy, even with all her problems, will be worked out by Him as well."

Another week had passed before Violet came to me and said, "That man did bad things to Lizzy."

"Which man, Violet?"

"She just said those brothers and overseer never fooled with her."

So, it's got to be the Judge himself and I kind of figured it could very well be him. That dirty rotten piece of dung!

When I went to Morgan with confirmation, he responded, "Vivian, the man is powerful, and he's gotten rid of many before me. He would rather keep on with his dirty secret than have a good doctor for his own family and others. Heaven help him if he ever gets sick or hurt!"

"Ham and Violet say this happens all the time with young slave girls. They just use them for their own gratification and then after a child is born, the child is treated just like any other slave. Will it ever stop?"

A few nights later, I had a dream, and in that dream, I was pregnant. Lord knows it's been a long time since I could have children, but it was so vivid, it gave me an idea that I could help Lizzy. After getting up that morning thinking about the dream, I ran down to where Morgan was putting up fences and told him I had a plan. "What's that Viv?"

"I will pretend to be expecting and when Lizzy's baby is born, I will say it's ours."

"But Vivian, it's bound to be black."

"Morgan, the Judge is blond haired/ blue eyed, and I have black hair with dark skin."

"Why can't we try it and if the child is too black, we can always say I lost the child?"

"I don't know Viv, I don't know."

"How are we going to explain a new baby any other way, will you tell me?"

"Well, I guess it's worth a try."

"Good, I'll go tell Violet and you tell Ham."

Cissy was back in school now that the snow had all but gone. She told me that she heard people talking about the runaway slave girl and how much reward there was for anyone who knew anything about it. She came home so afraid as she had gotten so attached to Ham, Violet and their children. I explained to her, "We must act like we know nothing, even if you have a best friend or Rev. Brooks can't know about this." Cissy promised to be silent.

Cissy was still teaching Noël, Jesse, and now Lizzy. She used one of the rooms on the third floor as a classroom. They had pencils, paper, and an old easel someone had left there. Whomever left the easel probably used it for painting, but she thought it was perfect for teaching letters and numbers.

The classroom was on the front side of the house so they could see if anyone rode up that might be checking on us for a number of reasons now. We all knew it was against the law for any slave to learn to read and write which made it even more exciting. They all learned quickly. Cissy was so proud of them for being able to write their names, ages, where they lived, etc. They could count to one hundred, spell some mighty big words, and now knew the meaning of many complex words which made them feel much smarter. Everyone was sworn to secrecy and knew the consequences if they let it slip.

CHAPTER 13

Dr. Banks

Now the tree was up, the stockings hung, and the baking had already begun with the children helping with the Christmas cookies. The Christmas service was going to be held this afternoon for those who lived so far away. The timing was also because there was a threat of snow again and that could create havoc getting back home safely. There were lighted candles in the windows and a tree was decorated up front in the church. A table was set up in the back with cookies, cake, and punch for anyone wanting to linger for a chat.

Our family was getting ready to go in when Judge Catron and his sons arrived yelling for us to wait up. The Judge motioned for the boys to go on inside and he said to me, "I haven't seen or talked to you since one of my slaves ran away and since you visit several homes I wondered if you had seen a young black girl around twelve years of age?"

"Well, I could have." I said, "But it didn't register since I wasn't looking for anyone. I can see a boy running, but why would a little girl run in the dead of winter? What did she do at your home?"

"Oh, she helped in the kitchen and things like that."

"Well, if I see anyone, course I see quite a few of those doing the same thing, I will keep my eyes open for you."

"Thanks Dr. Banks and you have a nice Christmas." Vivian and I rolled our eyes at each other after he left and proceeded into the church.

Vivian sang her usual two songs plus some Christmas carols. On the last song, Silent Night, she motioned for Ham to come in to play first and then the whole church joined in. Vivian and Ham truly made the service. This time the people complemented Ham as well as he went on out to wait in the wagon. The people really seemed to like our family, and everyone wished us a Merry Christmas.

We sang Christmas carols all the way home that late afternoon. A light snow began to fall about halfway there. Once inside Violet got a hot cup of coffee ready for everyone and hot chocolate for the younger folks. Violet had a big surprise for Noël, a huge birthday cake with four candles for each birthday they had missed. The cake was brought to the table with a present or two for her to open now, instead of tomorrow morning. Her brown eyes twinkled as she blew out her candles and made a wish. We pretended to be jealous that she got to open two presents now. After all what fun is it to open presents if everyone else is opening them too and it's your birthday?

"So, this is your special time little Noël, our special Christmas child." said Violet.

Everyone clapped and sang, "Happy birthday Christmas baby."

After our delicious Christmas Eve dinner with all the trimmings I said, "lets bow our heads in prayer." I prayed for the sick and the elderly who may not have as warm a house or as much good food as we did. And then I asked God to help them be able to keep their little girl, who had risked death from the cold by escaping into the night, not even knowing that her family was up at that house on the hill where she fled. "We believe that you God, led her to us and now we ask you to help us find a solution to this situation." And then I thanked Him for all the many blessings He had already given them. "We feel truly blessed Lord, in Jesus' name Amen."

Christmas and New Year's came and went. Soon the little girl was showing so anyone could tell. At this time Vivian began sewing little pouches and put them in front of her dress, then tied them in the back so she would look like she was expecting. She also knew that long through the summertime this could begin to be rather cumbersome and hot, but she was determined to see this through because what else could they do? How could they explain a new child? Anyone who came to the house would hear a baby cry. There were always people coming out to their house for various reasons, and you just had to invite them in for a cool drink. But since God was in control, He wouldn't want her worrying about it so much.

Violet decided Lizzy should get her hair out of pigtails to help her look different and rearranged Lizzy's hair in a style that made her look much older. Lizzy hated this but knew in order to be safe it had to be. Lizzy also got a pair of Vivian's glasses that were out of date. She was told to put these on if ever anyone came unexpectedly, and she didn't have a chance to hide. This really made her look plain when in fact, Lizzy was a very pretty girl. She looked like a different person altogether.

The rest of the winter was spent repairing and painting shutters. Ham carved out a pit in the backyard so they could roast meat on it. a whole pig if they wanted to. He loved doing things like that.

By spring they would have some three hundred acres fenced in, and they would use that leftover land to farm out for extra money. They had much more land than Judge Catron and his land joined theirs.

Again, Judge Catron rode out to get me to come to his house. "You know you said you didn't want me to come to your place again because I doctor the slaves."

"Yes, but I need you now cause the wife is screaming and yelling again!"

"Is she taking her medicine?"

"Yes, but the help is having a time getting it down her."

"Well Judge, I want to ask you a question?"

"Alright, be quick about it."

"Are you for me or against me?"

"What kind of question is that?"

"I mean are you going to try to run me out of town like you did the others?"

"Who said I did that?"

"Hey now, you know I see a lot of people. I'm not going to name every person I've treated and get them in trouble."

"No, I guess you wouldn't, but if you don't get to my house soon, they will have to tie her up."

"Ok, let's get moving."

When we arrived, we could hear her yelling from down the road. I went to her side the tears and could see tears had soaked through her dress. "Someone put some dry clothes on her and bring a cup of coffee."

She seemed to calm down when I began to talk. While they dressed her, I asked the Judge what he thought started these screaming and crying fits?

"I really don't rightly know." He had a look on his face that told me he sure did know.

Mrs. Catron wasn't a bad looking woman, in fact nicer looking than most. Which was easy to see now that she had calmed down considerably while I sat with her. "Now I'm going to up your medication, but if you get so you're just sitting and staring or sleeping more than staying awake, we will talk again. I know you are in a bad state of mind, but you can talk to me, and then maybe I can treat you with something different." She said nothing to me, just looked at me with big silent tears in her eyes and a hopeless look.

I left and told the Judge the same as I told his wife. When the Judge went back in to be with his wife, a maid came out to give me some food as payment. She whispered, "It's what she knows is going on here in her own house!" Then she hurried back inside.

Praying to God all the way home to help me do something about this situation was the best thing I knew to do in that moment. I knew this was going on in other homes as well and just wish I could find a way to help make it stop.

It makes me cringe when I think about how when they call the court to order, the Judge sits up there pretending he's worthy of the honorable part. He's looking the other way while these people are being whipped, and the women are being raped as young as ten (of which he himself is guilty). "Oh God, Oh God, what terrible ways are these?"

CHAPTER 14

Ham

Now that spring was coming, we needed more help, so it was time now to go into town and get a couple slaves to put all the crops in. A lot of plowing and planting to be done along with a good barn to be built for the new cows when they come and maybe another horse or mule. Dr. Banks asked me to stand beside him while he selected two able bodied men 'cause he thought maybe I would know them. "Where you gonna put these men, Dr. Banks?"

"Why in our house, of course."

"If I don't see any that I know, how you gonna decide?"

"Ham, I didn't know you. They told me you were a troublemaker and a runaway. I figured the two of you at such a low price was the wise thing to do. When Violet came out with little Noël hanging on to her for dear life, I couldn't resist them either thinking they could maybe be split up. Now let's just see what comes up."

Again, first up on the block was a young girl about twelve. The Judge thinking no one would see, got his overseer to bid. Then he grabbed her up real quick putting her in his wagon to run off with her. It gave me cold chills. Next up was a woman in her fifties and was supposed to be a good cook from a plantation that was downsizing. But we had enough women in our kitchen, too many at times.

After several women then came the men. There were five of them in all from the same plantation that was downsizing. I saw one I knew but hadn't heard too much good about him. The others I didn't know at all. Dr. Banks asked about their qualities and being shirtless anyone could see all but one of them had been whipped badly. He selected two of about the same age, one thirty and one close to forty. You had to pay a lot more for the younger ones. Dr. Banks said he could tell a lot by their eyes. He looked in the eyes of each of the men with these two having a more honest and pleading look. The others didn't look you in the eye and showed a little arrogance.

We went by the feed store on the way out of town and bought a few eggs as their hens were just starting to lay a few. With these two additional mouths to feed added to our table the women would need more.

When we arrived home the first thing Dr. Banks told the new men was as long as they did their job and caused no trouble they would work alongside him, eat with his family and sleep in their house. They would never be chained or whipped, and if they decided they wanted to leave just say so, but they also knew if they were spotted out there away from his land they would likely be shot or brought back to him. He also told them he didn't believe in slavery, and that they would be treated just like a white man if he had hired one. Buying them on the block is his way of freeing them so to speak, but they still work for him and get paid as well.

"Now Ham will show you to your rooms and what we are preparing to do with our land. We will start in the morning with an early breakfast and stop around one for lunch here at the house. Afterwards we will rest for an hour and a half to let your food digest then get back out to work. Being almost spring, we have light a little later which means we will work till six or so, and supper around seven. I know that sounds late, but in the winter months that will change, and we will come in about four forty-five. Don't go into town without one of our family with you, as that would cause us a lot of trouble. And above all never discuss what goes on here in our house or how you are treated. If anyone ever asks you about that, just say you are treated fairly."

Their chains were removed, and they were given a cool glass of tea or coffee with a piece of cake. Afterwards I took them to their bedrooms. They laid down their sacks then looked upon a real bed, a dresser and even a rug on the floor that Violet had woven out of rags. The puzzled look on their faces was worth a million dollars, and to have their own room was just plain unthinkable. They were used to ten or twelve to a room. One of the men, called Buck, said under his breath, "Praise Jesus."

I heard him and said, "You are two very lucky men, and you treat Dr. Banks with respect because I believe he be sent by God Himself."

After I left the men alone, I overheard them talking about what had just happened to them. First that they were ushered into the house right off the bat even though they knew they smelt like polecat, all dripping in sweat. Then that they all sat together sat at the family table. They were sure something's got to be wrong here and said, "Well, we'll see if he breaks our backs tomorrow!"

CHAPTER 15

Vivian

"Mrs. Vivvy," Violet said, as they stood at the stove cooking a much bigger breakfast than usual this morning. "I was just wondering; wouldn't it be better if I pretended to be the mother of this new baby coming? After all, it's my flesh and blood. That way if it be born dark skinned, we wouldn't have to be answering questions about that and it be easier to get a wet nurse if Lizzy don't get her milk."

"Well Violet, how come you figured that out and I didn't? You're not as dumb as I thought, but I was." And we laughed till we cried. "And it does make sense cause you are rounder than Lizzy or I and it won't show too much on you till closer to the birthing time."

"Now I will see what Ham says, but I'm sure he'll agree. And then you won't have to worry 'bout getting up and singing at Easter in church pretending."

"We really do need to sew her some more smocks as she is spreading in the waist. It's good that Cissy is keeping her occupied with books and learning."

CHAPTER 16

Jesse

I still rode out with Dr. Banks on most every trip, but the people didn't change and still treated me like I wasn't even human. If they could tell I really didn't need to assist the doctor, they made me stay in the wagon, but I was learning a lot about medicine and with Cissy's help a lot of other knowledge as well. I loved tending the animals and had asked Pa if he would build me a big henhouse? "How big?" asked Pa.

"Really big!"

"We'll have to ask Dr. Banks 'bout 'that big.'"

All of us men worked in the field planting wheat and potatoes. It was a little too early for corn. Dr. Banks wanted a hundred acres in wheat. Pa wanted a field of cotton too. Dr. Banks said Pa could use some land for that, but he and the other men would have to tend to it when they had time. Dr. Banks knew nothing about cotton.

Dr. Banks told us if we wanted to plow some of the ground down closer to the creek for a vegetable garden we could and then sell some of it at church or wherever. The money would be ours, but we alone would do the work on that.

We laid out plans for a barn and cut wood every day for what seemed like two weeks straight. With the five of us we had that barn going up in no time, and it was a beauty. It was large enough for several horses and twenty or more cows. I tell you it was a sight to see, a fine piece of work. We wanted to paint it another color besides red.

Dr Banks asked, "Well, what color?"

"Yellow, with green shutters," I yelled.

"Shutters?"

"Well, we will paint them on there, and make it look like there are windows on each side. That way it will look more like a house and an attraction for people to see."

And we did just that. People talked about it for weeks and were riding out to see for themselves, the barn with shutters! It did look nice. And proud? Oh my, we were puffed up for a long time, answering questions about "The Barn" and who made it.

The day the barn was finished everyone gathered under the big pecan trees and celebrated with a huge feast. There was lots of food, desserts, laughter, and a general all around wonderful mood we hadn't shown or even felt before. We were so proud of this accomplishment, and Dr. Banks paid us well for our efforts.

We were happy with our money and food that was fed to us. Pa told Buck, "It is pure Heaven on this hill."

"How could we have been so lucky to be chosen by Dr. Banks?"

"Dr. Banks don't figure it being luck at all."

"What do you mean?"

"He feels you have been chosen by God and sent to him because he prays for Him to send the people who have been mistreated the most so he can give them a better life. He believes that to those who are given much, being him, much is required of them. So, believe me, if you be thinking 'bout stealing from him, you be stealing from God Himself, so think twice."

Dr. Banks wrapped up the evening night saying, "Now we can begin to do some farming. We have five men here and two horses, so we need another horse because when Jesse rides out with me on a call, that leaves nothing for the rest of you to ride. This is a big place, and I don't expect you all to get from one place to another walking. We also need a few cows, hopefully one that already needs milking."

The following week as Dr. Banks and I were riding out to a call, Dr. Banks said, "Ham tells me you want a right good size henhouse."

"Yes sir Dr. Banks, that would be good."

"Is there something down the road you plan to do?"

"Yes, I is, I mean I am planning to make it a business."

"What do you figure you'll need?"

"Well, to start I'd say a long, low sort of thing with two stories, not too far off the ground. Pa could cut me some holes, one after another on the side and underneath so they can get out of the sun, shady like. I'm thinking something about forty yards long and about two feet deep. Then we'll pack the holes with straw and that'll be the nests."

"You know something that big can't be put close to the house. How you plan to make it safe for them from the wild animals?"

"Haven't thought much about that yet."

"Well, it sounds like a good money maker for you, but you need to think it through to the end. You have a few problems yet to figure out so get back to me when you consider everything. You may have something there Jesse, but I was hoping you wanted to become a doctor maybe."

"Well, that's kind of hard for me to think about. I can visualize this other life a little better."

"Cissy teaches you some big words there, visualize, just don't go using those big words around town folk or they'll be coming after me for sure."

"No sir I won't."

"Now don't you go thinking you can't become a doctor because by the time Cissy and I get through with you, you'll be able to do that and more. Right now, while you're still young, we'll see what this henhouse thing will do for you."

"Yes, sir I've loved those chicks since you got 'em. I like handling them and really the whole process."

"Watch those words Jesse in front of anyone outside our family. I'm afraid you're gonna slip up one of these days around the wrong people."

"I'll be careful Dr. Banks."

The people were still skeptical of Dr. Banks and especially what went on in the big house on the hill. There had been more talk about his treatment of the slaves and that he let them in his house. Now they could see the cook or maid with the children, but the fieldhands? When word gets around that some slaves are treated better, it causes others to be unhappy and become resentful which impacts their work.

Dr. Banks told Pa if he could make a henhouse look different and pleasing to the eye, Dr. Banks would ok him doing this. But Dr. Banks wanted to know if this was just a fleeting sort of notion that later he'd be left with and wouldn't have time for with it becoming an old, deserted eye sore. Pa told me he later he knew I was truly serious but wanted to have one more talk with me before agreeing to help.

CHAPTER 17

Dr. Banks

A man in town was saving me a horse knowing I would need it come spring and would pay top dollar. He raised her from birth, and she was a real beauty. We picked her up when we picked up the cows now that we had a place for them. Since she was nearing her first breeding time and we didn't want to breed her yet, we had a special fenced in area away from Barney and George.

We had to go slow on the way home because the cows were walking, and even though they were roped it wasn't easy keeping them in line at times. It was near dark when we were getting home and still a lot of work to be done. Jesse hurried and milked the one cow, and the rest were herded into the barn to be fed. They were all "plum wore out", as Ham put it. The horses, now fed and watered were ready to call it a day too.

The kittens, almost grown now, were shown the new barn. We hoped they would hang around there catching the mice and bugs. Instead, they wandered back up to the house which was home to them for so long. They loved the children and wandered all through the house anytime they pleased.

This new group of animals meant more work for each man. They sat that night after prayers and decided who needed to do what.

The women were excited about having fresh milk and the aroma of fresh bread through the house was enough to make you gather in the kitchen to wait for a warm slice with butter and jam. The two new men had not been told about the events leading up to the girl coming to the house in the night. Somehow Ham and I felt they would wait until they knew these men better, but so far, they seemed a decent sort.

Even with all the excitement of farm life, not being able to treat the slaves in the area continued to lay heavy on my heart knowing they needed medical attention. But I just couldn't seem to get the council to let me practice in town if I did this. So, I decided to go to the council when they held their next meeting.

When time came for me to get up and speak the room all of a sudden became very quiet. I never raised my voice and spoke with authority which you could tell the Judge didn't like at all.

"Now you all know I came down here first to practice medicine and second to farm. Why wouldn't any of you want your slaves to be healthy? Why wouldn't any of you not want someone helping deliver them with healthy babies? What would you do if I refused to treat your children or your wives? I have heard that in the year or two before I came you had many deaths. Any of you had a child or wife or mother to die lately? Now I ask you once more to let me set up my practice in town so I can reach more of the sick and yes, treat the slaves and their families too."

One of the councilmen responded with, "We hear you put no restrictions on your slaves, and they go about the place like they have no owner or overseer."

"Do I tell you how to treat your slaves? I treat my slaves fairly, and I pay them well for their work. Now even though I deplore what some of you do with your slaves, beating and raping them, I do not come to you and tell you I will not treat you because you do these horrible things. I am just a doctor who took an oath and that was to treat all people who are sick or need my attention. I don't pick who I will or won't see. Now the only thing I will tell you is I can let the slaves come through a different door to the clinic and that way you won't see them most of the time. The clinic is also for the white folks who live and work in or close to town but who don't have a way to come out to my home to get me. Now what's it going to be gentleman? And yes, I will bring my assistant who is black, to the clinic to help me along with my wife from time to time."

"Why the boy slave?"

"First because I need his help; second because he has a strong arm and can lift some of the elderly or folks who for some reason can't walk. Also, he has a sharp mind and aspires to be in medicine one day. He does not flinch when he sees blood, has a steady hand and a way that calms folks."

"But he's a damn slave!"

"I won't reply to that narrow-minded remark! Do I have a clinic or not? If not, I may decide to be a full-time farmer and will not, I say will not, treat anyone. Remember this, I do know a lot about you people on council and more about the Judge if that helps sway your decision. I will go now, and I expect an answer, yes or no, within a reasonable period. The fact that you haven't had a death except for a stillborn child and two elderlies ready to die of old age people since I have been here should help you make up your mind as well. The black people are afraid to come get me to treat them. That must stop for your county to thrive and survive. When a black man, woman, or child dies, they get a death certificate just like the white people and their births are recorded as well. That should tell you they are human. I'll go now and await your reply."

At church the next day no one sat near the Banks family, and Vivian was not asked to sing. Everyone filed out without saying one word to them. Cissy said, "Daddy why are they treating us like this?"

"Because I went before the Judge and council yesterday about the clinic in town and treating the slaves."

"I thought they were not asking you to treat anyone."

"Who? The council and Judge?"

"Yes, I thought the Jude forbade the councilmen to call on you for help."

"That's right, but some of them have anyway. That's where the rub is. The Judge is asking them to not do something that he is doing."

"Well, that's unfair!"

"Yes, it is and that's who this county's Judge is, dishonest to the core along with other horrible things I might add."

"But his son Jeff is so nice. If he had been here today, he would have spoken to me."

"Don't be too sure about that."

"Daddy, he's nice."

"Ok, if you say so. Now let's buy a few things and get out of here."

They talked on the way home about what the Judge would do when his wife's medicine runs out. The question is what am I going to do when her medicine runs out?

It was about ten days before I got a reply and was asked to come back in front of the council. Their answer was yes, but it had stipulations attached. There were to be no black people lined up in the street. They would come and go through the back door. They could not borrow money from their owner to pay me and if I kept them off work for more than a couple of days, there would be "hell" to pay!

To this last requirement I responded, "Now hold on here, these people get the measles or break their arms or worse, just like any other, and when I say they need to be quarantined, I mean that, or we will have an epidemic on our hands. Also, when I feel it's necessary to bring them to my house to keep a closer watch on them, I want that allowed to, just as I would you or any of your family. And I do not want to be responsible for them before they get to the clinic or after they leave, only if I take them home with me for a recuperation period."

"Well, this brings up another problem then, and that's who is going to take them to you then wait on them to take them back?"

"If you're smart, your overseer or another slave that you trust. That's pretty much your problem, but let me ask you, what's more important, a healthy slave or a dead slave? You pay good money for what you hope is a healthy slave when you buy him, so you don't need to lose that money for something a little bit of medicine can fix. Do you want to vote again while I'm here or do you want me step outside?"

The Judge said for me to step outside. So, I sat out under a shady tree for about thirty minutes before they called me back. They made one remark, "If you take a man home and he runs away, what happens then?"

"First of all, he won't be in any shape to run if he is sick enough for me to take him home, and he will be returned to you way before he feels like running again, as well."

"Ok, we hold you responsible for that. Deal?"

"Yes, it's a deal."

So that was that, finally an ok to proceed with my practice. On the way home I tried to figure what all I would need to do first to get started. I would have to talk to Mr. McBroom first thing to see if there were any new places that had come up since the last time I talked with him. I actually needed four or five rooms. One for a treatment room, one for operating, one for the waiting room, one for an office, and storage space for my supplies that I could combine with the office if necessary. Then I need to order my supplies right away because they take a while to get here, sometimes even a month and even then not everything I orders comes.

A first come first serve basis would work best for the clinic unless one of the town's people came by and said they wanted to be seen Monday at three which would be fine. If any emergency came in that would always come first and I would have to let them know that. The clinic would be opening starting with Mondays and Thursdays to see how many patients I saw, then that might have to change. I needed the other days for farming.

Now to keep the people separated there would have to be chairs along one side of the room for blacks and the other side for whites. Maybe a room divider might work too, like a big center wooden piece of furniture with plants on top to make it taller? It would have to be a pretty good size room and maybe Ham could come up with something nice that he could make. I had mixed emotions about how all this would work out, but at least I could see more people this way.

Mr. McBroom was able to find a place for the clinic after about a week and papers were ready for me to sign on a piece of property about a hundred yards from town, a corner spot on the end of a building. It's perfect this way because the people won't see everybody coming in and out of my office so easy. I am concerned about window space though. In the summertime those people will burn up sitting in there for more than a half hour. There is only one window in that room that has to be the waiting area. Oh well, you can't have it all. I'll need a couple white coats and maybe one for Jesse, not necessarily white but something to help him look professional. I'll have to see if Vivian or Violet can make me those, if not I'll have to order them.

CHAPTER 18

Vivian

I don't know who is bigger, Lizzy or her mother. They have packed those chicken feathers inside that pouch so tight I'm afraid they're gonna come poking out through her dress one of these days. We let Violet go into town with us so everyone would notice she was expecting, but poor Lizzy has not been able to be seen because it's only been six months or so since she ran away. It was still fresh on the minds of a lot of people, including the Judge's and the folks that would like the reward money. Ham and Violet are just happy to have her back safe. I worry, safe but for how long?

Ham said he would make chairs for the clinic. Violet and I would make curtains and cushions for the chairs. Counting all the trips back and forth to town, which took a lot of hours out of a day especially with the unloading the wagon each time, cleaning out the rooms (a clinic should be always clean from top to bottom), making the rooms bright and cheerful, stocking the shelves with supplies and making charts to keep the information on each patient, all took about a month.

Once the clinic opened, Jesse came with Morgan each time and dressed in a nice shirt with tie. Morgan could not have done without him because some came lying in wagons and had to be lifted on the examining table.

Also, Morgan soon found out none of the slaves could afford treatment. But he figured that out ahead of time and just let it slide because he didn't want them getting in trouble asking their owners for money to pay him. He wasn't planning on making any kind of profit from them anyway.

Although Ham and Violet worked well together caring for each other, there was always a sadness in their eyes when they thought no one was looking. I said to Morgan one morning, "There is something missing, and we know what it is." It was their other daughter who they believed to still be at the Judge's house but weren't sure anymore.

That night's prayers which were held outside now because it was still light till around eight-thirty some evenings, and tonight was a lovely night to be out. Morgan said, "Let's all join hands and ask God to bring Ham and Violet's only other child, Esther, to them. We are praying for her especially tonight because of the heaviness on their hearts." We prayed silently and openly about this praising God for already answering our prayer because He said, "when two or more of you are gathered together in My name, your prayers will be answered." We all went to bed that night believing that Esther would be returned to them someday and soon.

Several weeks later the dogs were barking loudly. Morgan heard them first and then so did the other men. He got his lamp then lit it and rushed to the door. It was Martin, Judge Catron's son, screaming for him to come quick. The son told him to follow him to the creek which ran behind Morgan's and the Judge's land. When they got there Mrs. Catron was on the ground and Morgan got no pulse at all. "When did you find her?"

The Judge said, after dinner he couldn't find her in the house and looked outside. Finally, he got his overseer and a couple of his men to look in every direction. When his overseer found her, she was face down in the swollen creek and he didn't know how long she had been like that. They moved her on back to the house, which was a good way from where they found her. When Morgan talked to the maid, she said, "let me clean her up and we will talk a little later" and then whispered, "alone." The sons were obviously distraught, but the Judge was stone-faced and anything but sad.

The funeral was the next day, and there was an overflow crowd. I sang two moving songs, and being summertime, there were many flowers. She was laid to rest in the church cemetery.

On the way home from the funeral, Morgan told me there was something fishy here. He would find out sooner or later from the maid that took care of Mrs. Catron for many years, just what went on that night. Since there was no proof of what really happened that night, Morgan went on and posted the death certificate with her death ruled accidental.

CHAPTER 19

Lizzy

Cissy and I were exploring some of the many rooms in the house. One day we came across a section of stone that was on both sides of the fireplace but I noticed on one of these sections there was a latch at the bottom near the floor. I'd seen this before in another house I was a slave in before so I unlatched it, opened inward, and when we closed it you couldn't tell where it opened. Cissy immediately said, "This must be some secret hiding place!"

I was scared of what they might find in there as I had seen and experienced so many dark things in my life, but Cissy squeezed my hand and reminded me I wasn't alone anymore. We had to almost crawl into the place, and I placed an old rag in the crack so it wouldn't close on us. Because there were no windows we could hardly see at all so Cissy said, "I'm going back to light a lamp."

"And I'll go with you."

"Oh Lizzy, there's no one in there."

I was not letting Cissy out of my sight so when we came back with a lamp, we were amazed at all the stuff hidden in that little space. A chest, several pillowcases stuffed with who knows what. A tin or two, one with jewelry and oh my goodness, the other had money in it. Not just coins but bills.

Before we went any further, we ran to get Mrs. Banks. We showed her the money and all the other things we had found. Mrs. Banks sat down outside the little crawl space and counted the money.

CHAPTER 20

Vivian

When the girls showed me what they found in the hidden room I tried not to really excited because I didn't want them to know how much was there until I told Morgan later that evening after he got home from the clinic. I went back to canning with Violet and kept on till we finished. Beans, squash, peppers, and cucumbers were all coming in at the same time, not to mention tomatoes and peas. The corn would be ready soon too. We put up pickles and relish, oh what a busy time in the kitchen."

Before lunch I went looking for the girls wondering why I couldn't get them in there to help. But they were busy too, busy going through all that stuff they found upstairs. Naturally Noël was interested in whatever the big girls were doing and she did her best to help but I think she was more in the way than helpful.

That evening Morgan had brought a bushel of peaches home with him that one of his patients had given him as a payment. They have to be peeled and canned soon, probably by tomorrow as they are fully ripe. Now with ten mouths to feed, soon be eleven, it would take Cissy and Lizzy to help the Violet and me to can all these peaches.

Before we could get started on the peaches, I had to take Morgan aside after the girls kept yelling and screaming about the money they found. "Can we keep it, Daddy?"

"Well, let's just see what this is all about."

I told him where they found it first and then the astonishing amount of four hundred dollars. "My heavens," said Morgan, "before we decide anything we'll have to see if there's a letter among the things in there telling us anything about it."

"Why would anyone leave that kind of money and not give it to someone rather than leave it hidden away for strangers to find?"

When he saw the trick wall beside the fireplace and an old wood box covering the latch on the floor, he said, "that's the strangest thing I have ever seen. This was no doubt the owner's bedroom."

"And the jewelry too, Morgan, those are nice pieces and worth a pretty penny."

The girls searched all the next morning for clues as to why these things were hidden away (so much for helping can peaches). They found an old wedding dress, baby pictures and a family portrait. In the family pictures there appeared to be three sons.

Cissy eventually found a letter with no name on the front and brought it to me. I opened it and read that the husband had died. She had become ill and was treated poorly by her sons' wives while her sons were out doing their jobs. When she told her sons, they didn't believe her. No one knew about the hidden room, and she said she would never leave her belongings to anyone that treated her so badly. She would rather a perfect stranger be the recipient of all she had. Her last wish was that whoever found the room to put what they found to good use and enjoy because she asked God to give it to someone who would be a good steward. She knows He would answer her prayer.

Oh my, I cried, "Lord, we certainly will try to honor her wishes."

"What about finders, keepers?" Cissy asked a little later.

Morgan said, "With this letter explaining what she wanted done with her money and things, we will have to make sure it is used in the right way, but I will give you and Lizzy a couple of dollars each because you did find it. The rest of it will go to good causes. One thing I have in mind is for our church."

I found it strange that the letter was not signed properly. It just said, Maureen H. and I supposed that was the Hudson family that lived here some eight or ten years ago. So why didn't she go ahead and write her last name? We will have to look into this a little further. Really sounds strange to me. Morgan see a good number of patients, surely somebody knows something about that family. We know she had three sons, and she was mistreated by their wives, but how about grandchildren? Were there any and if so, where were they?

CHAPTER 21

Dr. Banks

Jesse and I worked as hard at the clinic. On this day I had a surprise patient. It was the maid from the Judge's house. She came not as a patient but to talk about the night Mrs. Catron died.

"I was afraid to get even close to you that night Dr. Banks, 'cause the Judge knows I hear things, and the missus told me a lot. The missus loved her husband, and they had a good marriage at first. She knew 'bout him always messin' with the new young slaves he brought home, and it drove her to be like she was. He brought them right in his house to his room. You see the Judge and the missus had separate rooms. One of the doctors before you told her she may not make it through another delivery, so the Judge decided to have his own room. She would get up in the night and hear him from the hall. It made her sick. She wouldn't leave her room for days and hardly eat. On that last night that she died, I had stayed with her because she seemed much worse. She got up twice that night and came back hysterical, saying he had two different ones in there. She said she couldn't take it anymore, so she went to his door and opened it. Sure enough there were two of them and he was all over that youngin' no more than eleven or twelve years old. She told the girl to get out. 'Leave! I will not take this anymore.' The missus came over and jerked that child out of the bed. I wouldn't have thought she had the strength, but she was so upset, she didn't know how much strength she had. Then the Judge slapped the missus and told her to get out, 'Go to your room!' I was standing in the hall and wrapped that child up and told her to get. They argued all through the house. The boys were there, I know they could hear. Then the Judge told her to get out and she said 'No, this is my father's house, and it belongs to me.' Then the Judge said, 'Well while I live here, I am the head of this house, and you get out.' Then after he pushed her through the door and locked it, he poured himself another drink. I didn't hear another thing 'till I heard him call his boys and say, 'Go get your mother. She's run away. She's gone completely mad!' That's what I saw that night Dr. Banks. He was a cruel man. He coulda done his bad business somewhere else, not right under her nose."

"Well, anywhere else would have been too easy for folks to find out about him."

"He drove the missus insane, and I hate him for it."

"Thank you for telling me this, and I will give you some sugar pills to take back home with you. If he questions you about it, just tell him you saw me for an earache, ok? I will put that in your chart in case he comes here snooping around and wants proof."

"Yes sa Dr. Banks, and one day if anything happens to you, I may have to be a witness."

"I don't think it will ever come to that. Besides we really can't prove anything except that you saw him lock her out. You didn't see him go out there and do anything to her, so we must let it be. We can't prove a thing. But we do know that he's the one who should have been thrown out that night. He may be a Judge in this life, but there is a higher Judge who will, shall we say, throw the Book at him when he dies."

"Yes sa, Dr. Banks, you be right 'bout that."

"Now let me ask you a question. The day I bought four slaves on block, soon after moving down here, the Judge bought two young girls and drove away immediately. That was back almost in the middle of June. The one I saw bleeding so badly that night and the runaway, are they sisters?"

"Yes, sa and she still be there."

"Oh my."

"How many young girls does he have there now?"

"Oh, I'd say about four now; most live out back with the others. Some are older, like fifteen and eighteen now, but he messes with all of 'em. It's a sad thing sa and they can't do nothing 'bout it."

"I know it's a horrible thing."

"I hate it and can't stop it. He has kids by most of them, course several died, being so young and all. We had no doctor to help."

"Now he wouldn't call on me to help, because I would know too much about his business. Thank you for coming here today, and one day we will straighten this out, or I should say God will. Would you like to leave now that Mrs. Catron has gone?"

"Oh, Dr. Banks, he would never let me go. I know too much, but I would love to be up there on the hill with all you. I hear it's too good to be true up there."

"Maybe one day soon you will get your wish."

It was a good thing I stayed on the farm the next day because around noon Cissy ran to the barn to get me calling, "Lizzy is doubled over in pain, Daddy. I think it's her time."

It was a struggle for this child, and I'm surprised she carried the baby to term. The baby was a big one, too big for our little Lizzy. He was here and he was fine, all eight and a half pounds of him. I did keep her in bed for ten days and she seemed fine after that, course we took good care of her. She didn't want for anything. Cissy fed her every meal in bed and even gave her books to read to keep up with her lessons. It was a happy time.

Violet took off her pouch and took real good care of her grandbaby. This whole thing seemed to help sooth some of the hurt of not having her other daughter here. She told Viv that she knew God was working it all out even though she still prayed day and night for her Esther to be released to them somehow.

HEAVEN ON THE HILL

CHAPTER 22

Cissy

Violet found a wet nurse from a community not far from us. Daddy had to pay well for her because she was a slave, and her owner didn't want her to leave. The money and Daddy being the doctor around here had a lot to do with her owner agreeing to do it. In two months, the baby was switched to cow's milk since it agreed with him, so the slave was sent back, but we had a time trying to pretend that the baby boy belonged to Violet and Ham. He had light skin and green eyes so Mommy could have easily gone ahead with her plans at the beginning to pretend he was hers. I would have loved having a little brother. Cissy named him Nathaniel.

We looked for weeks for clues to the hidden treasures we found but nothing surfaced so Mommy and Daddy decided to do several things with the money. The first thing happened a few weeks later when we went to church as usual, and before the pastor began to speak he called 'brother Morgan' to the podium.

Daddy said, "All in all the town and its people have been good to me and my family, especially our church family. Our clinic is doing well, and the slaves of this county may have their own doctor here in a couple of years, which would be a first. Because of your kindness, I, and my family would like to express our gratitude by

85

donating a new piano for the church, which should arrive in a few weeks."

There was a standing ovation. Mommy got up to sang and there was not a dry eye in the church. She had many talents and I hoped one day I could grow up to be more like her. We brought pies and cakes for the entire congregation to celebrate the new piano after the service was over. The people stayed for an hour afterwards, thanking us for such a marvelous gift.

Summer was almost over, which meant the wheat was harvested and corn along with most everything else was picked or dug up. We had another barn dance the last week of summer. I couldn't stop thinking or talking about Jeff, and he had asked me to be his girl. We danced nearly every dance together. When the dance was over, we didn't see each other but once a week after church for about thirty minutes. I thought about him constantly, but I could tell Mommy and Daddy were not too sure about this love between us. That would change once they knew him like I did.

CHAPTER 23

Vivian

We knew too much about Jeff's family, and it was the last thing we wanted for our only daughter to be involved with a Catron. But Cissy talked about him constantly, and young love is very strong. Jeff knew she was too young for him to come courting, but they would meet down at the road every now and then to stand by the gate to the barn.

While we watched over those two, Morgan and I would sit outside under a tree talking about our love for each other along with all our other blessings. We loved what we were doing. Cissy, our only child, had made us so proud teaching the slaves to read and write. Our hope was that she would continue to go to school and become a teacher, but we were fearful right now that she may be so smitten with this Catron boy that she would put all her dreams aside for him. He seemed nice enough but coming from a family like Judge Catron's was frightening, knowing all we knew. And even though this young man attended church, so did his father. Could he be a Christian? How could we know if we didn't get to know him a lot better?

Jeff & Cissy seemed to only have eyes for each other, and they met as often as they could. Jeff couldn't wait to come to see her at home to sit with her and find out more about her family and what went on up at the house on the hill.

So just before Cissy turned sixteen, Jeff asked if he could talk to Morgan about something after church. He wanted to know if he could come and court Cissy. Morgan said, "I don't mind if you come to the house to do your courting, but it's too far to go into town." He forbade him to take her to his house.

Once Jeff was officially courting Cissy, he started coming to our house a couple times a week. They would stay in the sitting room talking and looking at each other with excitement. The rest of the people in the house left them alone, and we certainly didn't want him to wander through the house to find out more about the life we live here. It was a strain on us to say the least. Morgan and I only wished there were more young men to choose from around here.

CHAPTER 24

Dr. Banks

Big John, one of the last two men that came to work for us, had fallen for a girl from another community on the other side of town and he asked me if he could bring her here as his wife. I asked, "Is there no black church with a minister over there?"

"No sa, but this be a mighty fine woman and a good worker too."

"Do you know who she works for or who owns her?"

"Yes sa."

"Well, I'll have to go and speak to him about this and see what we can do."

"That be good Dr. Banks."

About a week later I rode up to this fellow's small farm to make a deal for the young lady. The owner was not that pleased to see me and I hadn't treated any of his family, so this was going to be a tough negotiation.

The owner started off complaining, "Well, this girl Peaches, hasn't been worth a plug nickel since she hooked up with that slave of yours! Do you just let your slaves run here and there? Aren't you afraid they'll run away?"

"No, I'm not. They ask if they can go, they tell me where they're going and they know when to be back."

"Well, I never heard of such a thing! Now the only way I'll let her go is if you pay for her just like you would if she were on the block. Now since I could have bred her with one of my own and hope for a boy to raise up as a worker, I'll be asking right much."

"Say your price mister and we'll be done here." I gladly paid the amount, and the girl didn't say a word till they got a short distance from the farm, and she had a smile on her face that lasted till I had her home. On the way I asked, "Do you know where you're going young lady?"

"Yes sa, I be going to your place called 'Heaven on the Hill.'"

"Now why do they call my place that?"

"I don't know sa, my man says that's what Ham calls it."

My smile was almost as big as hers when she told me that. God really is so good.

The wedding was held the next day. Apparently, their wedding vows are just words chosen for each other with family and friends as witnesses to their union since none of us was a pastor. It was a beautiful little ceremony, and we had a wonderful reception for them out under the big pecan trees with white tablecloths and flowers on each table. We served all kinds of food along with the wedding cake that Violet made, which was simply delicious as usual. We chose a room for them on the far side of the house for a little privacy. We grew to love this smiling young lady who was sweet as peaches.

One day not too long after the wedding, I asked her how she came to have a name like Peaches. She said picking peaches was her main job because she could pick a bushel quicker than anybody, so when they lined up every morning the overseer would call out what we be doing that day and when he pointed to her, he just said, "peaches" and she knew that was her job.

"Well things will be a little different here since we don't have a peach orchard. What is it you like to do most, other than pick peaches?"

"Well sa, Dr. Banks, they let me work now and then in the kitchen for the big suppers and I love to fry chicken. I do that real good."

"Very well then, we shall see if you can top Violet's fried chicken. If you can, that will be one of your jobs here. But you got to prove it."

"Yes sa Dr. Banks, I can do it."

It was hard for the love birds to pull away from each other in the mornings, but after a few weeks things settled down.

Little Nat was a great big baby and young Noël was getting to be old enough to help her older sister take care of him. Jesse and Lizzy were good pupils and learned fast, but it was hard for them to hold back the things they knew when around others. At least it was for Jesse. Jesse was anxious to get started on his henhouse and he had the plans all drawn up.

Ham was pretty much the overseer of the place because I was at the clinic more and more. When Jesse couldn't come with him, Viv would, and it was nice to have a little alone time on the rides into the clinic with her. Besides the female patients felt more comfortable with her if it was a female problem. Viv had always been my assistant before we came here anyway.

Jesse still loved medicine, but you know young people like to do it all at one time. I was the same way. He was just itching to get the henhouse up, hens laying and turning a profit. So, he, Ham, Buck, and Big John started on it. With all four of them working on it together, it didn't take much more than a week to get everything in operation. The fencing took a while, and they got some chickens from the henhouse up close to the main house on the hill. They had so many chickens already that there really was no need to buy more. Eventually we would tear down the one up at the house anyway.

Ham can build anything, but Jesse wasn't at all talented in that way. Oh, he could hammer a nail or down a tree and chop wood but to make a table or a stool; he just didn't have it. People would ride by and look at the new henhouse but really couldn't tell what it was from a distance. It didn't look like anyone else's henhouse, that's for sure. Jesse was so proud. It was a business venture for him, and he planned to make some money and of course I encouraged that.

I hoped Ham would start making furniture to sell it in town, so he could have his own side business too. Unfortunately, Ham was so busy with his cotton and other chores that he couldn't find the time and was too exhausted at days end. As we get older we just can't go like we used to. Maybe someday because he really did have talent and could open his own business one day when they allowed blacks to do that or I would open it for him and of course give him all the profits. These were real fine people and we wanted them all to prosper.

CHAPTER 25

Jesse

One stormy night after raining for a day and a half, looking out the windows after I heard the dogs barking I saw a man riding up to the house. It was dark so I couldn't tell who it was until the man came up to the door. Dr. Banks called out that Jeff was here and worried because he hadn't seen his dad come home that evening. Jeff was worried something had happened to him considering the weather and said his brother was out looking for him too.

The Big Black River was higher than it had ever been and there was mud and water everywhere. Jeff was pretty sure his dad was in trouble because it wasn't like him to come home that late. Dr. Banks, me and Big John rode out with Jeff to see if we could help find the Judge. We stayed on the road he would have come home on but saw nothing. Just when we were soaked to the bone and ready to turn back we spotted his wagon on the familiar road with a tree fallen on the wagon and he there he was pinned under the trunk.

Right away Dr. Banks saw that this was not a good situation. He told us that we would have to cut the tree to get it off him so Big John rode back to get the saws and hurried back. Dr. Banks always brought his bag when he rode out on any call, and it was a good thing because the man was suffering and no telling how long he had been stuck like this. Dr. Banks gave him something for pain and once Big John was back we all began sawing in two places. Then the four of them lifted the tree off the body.

Jeff stayed close saying as bravely as he could, "You're going to be ok, Dad." Big John & I lifted the Judge into the wagon, covered him, then we all set out for the Catron house. The other son had been home just a little while and was waiting with the rest of the staff to do what was necessary. Dry clothes and hot water were ready for sterilization and everything else they could think of. We put him up on the table and Dr. Banks examined him from head to toe. His pulse was very faint, and he had no feeling in his legs at all. Dr Banks feared he was without circulation in his legs too long and with that a terrible blow to the head, his chances of surviving were slim to none.

Dr. Banks worked on him through the rest of the night into the morning and never left his side. The Judge lived twenty-four hours after they found him which is twenty-three hours more than he would have if we had not helped him. Dr. Banks told them if he had lived, he would have had to amputate both legs plus he wasn't sure if maybe the lightening hadn't struck him and the tree at the same time. It was just a terrible freak accident.

The Judge was buried the following day beside Mrs. Catron in the church cemetery. It was still raining and the ground nothing but mud when they left. Few people were there. Could have been the weather.

CHAPTER 26

Dr. Banks

Things were good on the hill and the crops were doing well. Ham's cotton was sold at market for a good price. Jesse's hens were producing a record number of eggs which were sold in town and on Sunday after church. Both men were more than pleased with the money they were making.

But I couldn't let up on Jesse's studies just because he was having success in one area of his life. As I had learned myself, life is fuller if you have more than one occupation to keep you busy. Since being able to read better, I bought Jesse books to read about medicine and even let him do minor surgery at the clinic. I had a gut feeling that Jesse could and would one day be a great doctor.

There was still talk about Cissy and Jeff. I didn't know how to discourage her from this union. Anything I would say would hurt her feelings. Even now without the Judge being there I still didn't feel this was the right thing for my daughter. If I could just encourage her to wait a while. But sometimes when you try to make them wait; it only leads to a worse situation than you had before. Young love is so strong, and Jeff could lead her to do something she would forever regret.

There seemed to be nothing I could do, and Jeff really doesn't know all that's going on in our house. He knows nothing of the slaves living with us or the runaway slave of his father's, being here. Cissy and Lizzy are as close as sisters and if he found out that slave belonged to his father it would make her really his slave now. Too many bad things could come of this, but at this love-struck time in Cissy's life, even all that wouldn't keep her from being with her man.

And the very day Cissy became seventeen, Jeff rode up to the house with a gift in his hand and wanted to speak to me first. I had a pretty good idea what he wanted to ask me but I still was not sure what to say in return. How could I say no and break Cissy's heart? Jeff said, "Dr. Banks, I would like your permission to ask Cissy to marry me."

"Well, my boy, I figured as much, and I have only this to say; that you treat her with love and kindness. She is my only child and I want no harm to come to her, ever, or you will have me to reckon with and everyone else up here on the hill."

"Yes sir, and thank you, sir," and then Jeff ran to find Cissy.

After Jeff left the house that day I told Cissy I wanted us to have a little chat after supper. At the supper table when I said grace, I asked God to bless this union between Cissy and Jeff and ask that their marriage be successful, happy and God centered. Everyone was happy for her, but Viv and I still had reservations about the whole thing. Something just didn't feel right. I wanted to feel good about it, but I couldn't so I convinced myself that most parents had those same feelings about who their children marry. I would try to accept it and go on.

When Cissy came to me after dinner we went outside on the porch and sat in the big ole chairs that Ham had made with the big stuffed cushions that Violet sewed for them. You could just sit and waste a whole day out there in those easy chairs plus it made these hard conversations a little easier.

"What was it you wanted to talk about, Daddy?

"Cissy, you being our only child, I guess we worry a lot more about you than if we had several children, but then I guess we would worry just the same over each one, no matter how many. What I'm trying to say is, I know you are the happiest you have ever been, and I don't want you to think I'm trying to take that away from you especially on a day like today, with a pretty ring on your finger and all, but I can't help feeling that it's too soon for you to marry. I know you have been seeing Jeff for a good while, but do you really know him?"

"Yes Daddy, how could I know him any better than I do right now?"

"Well, we have this secret of ours about the living arrangement here in our house and I don't know just how he would take our particular circumstances. I also heard you tell your mother that you wanted Lizzy to be in your wedding. You know by all rights Lizzy belongs to Jeff and his brother now since they inherited everything from the Judge which goes for his slaves too."

"Well Daddy, Jeff has seen Lizzy here at the house in the kitchen and he said nothing."

"She looks entirely different now and they didn't call her Lizzy while she was at Judge Carton's house. Are you planning on telling Jeff that you want Lizzy as your maid of honor?"

"I'm not sure yet Daddy."

"Well, you tell me then why you are not sure Cissy. You must base your marriage on honesty and trust with each other. You know that, right?"

"Yes, but Jeff doesn't always talk so nice about black people or slaves and I am afraid he would get angry with me."

"Cissy, that's why I'm telling you, you may not know him as well as you should. You have very different views on life issues and our customs."

"Daddy, I don't want to talk about this anymore and I'm not planning to tell Jeff about Lizzy being in my wedding. I must have her because she is my best friend, and she would be so sad if she weren't a part of the ceremony. But he would say no about that and I'm not prepared to deal with it right now."

"Cissy, it's better to get it out of the way before the wedding, not after. I would understand him being angry that you didn't tell him knowing his views about slaves, even though I disagree with his views."

"Please Daddy, I don't want to talk about it, ok? Let me be happy. Besides I have no one else to be my maid of honor, and Lizzy is my family. I love her. Jeff will have to accept that, and he'll get over it."

"Cissy, I want what you want, but I have to tell you, you are not doing the right thing in this case."

"The wedding is not tomorrow, maybe I'll think of something before that time comes."

The next few weeks were busy for everyone, making plans about what to wear and what to cook for the wedding. Cissy was wearing her mother's wedding dress with a new veil that Viv was making. Also, Lizzy was wearing a pale blue long dress with a little short matching veil made by her mother, and both would carry fresh flowers from their flower garden tied with matching ribbons streaming down.

They needed to get all these things done to concentrate on the food the last two days before the wedding. That was going to be a job making sure they had enough food for the huge crowd they were expecting. They would use the clinic to store some of their things and food too.

Violet told Viv she wished she and Ham could see their lovely daughter walk down the aisle to stand by Cissy. But Violet would get to see her all dressed and pretty before and after the wedding. Everyone would also help set up and serve the food afterwards at the reception. Violet needed a nice dress too and she would sew it herself with a little help from Vivian. Ham would wear a white shirt and one of my pairs of dark pants.

If the weather was nice, they would have an outdoor service under the trees behind the church, if not, inside where hopefully it wouldn't be so hot since the place would be packed on this exciting day. Violet was making little white fans with ribbons on them for the ladies in case it was a scorcher of a day. Instead of invitations being sent, the minister would tell the congregation on Sunday, two weeks prior to the wedding that everyone was invited and there would be food for all who came. Also, I would tell several of the town's people that they were invited as well, even if they didn't attend our church.

The wedding of Cecilia Banks and Jeffrey Catron was held in the church with the whole countryside attending, some had to stand in the foyer of the church. When Lizzy walked down the aisle everyone gasped! Jeff standing down front looked horrified when he saw her come down and stand in front with him. But she did look absolutely beautiful and smiled the whole time.

CHAPTER 27

Cissy

My heart was racing as I walked down the aisle to be with my husband. I was so excited but when he looked over at me all he said was, "I have never heard of such a thing," obviously mad.

"Well do you want me or not?"

"Of course, I do, but this is going too far."

"She's my best friend. We have grown up together and feel like sisters."

"Well, she's not your sister!"

I had never seen him act like this and on our wedding day! He had me almost in tears during the ceremony. The reception was held in the church yard and there was music, laughter, too much food, and then the cake. What a beautiful cake! Violet had done a tremendous job and how they traveled with it and not messed it up, was the question of the year. Mommy cried about how beautiful I looked as a young bride.

Both Mommy and Daddy seemed to finally be happy now that I appeared to be happy after all. Jeff was all I could think about for the last four years and now it was finally true. I couldn't wait to move to the Catron house & start to make it our home.

During this time I also became the teacher for the town's only school, with grades one through twelve. I had finally become what I had dreamed about, Jeff's wife and a teacher. I vowed I wouldn't ignore the slaves and would teach them in my spare time if and when they could get away from their work. But I knew my job was at stake if anyone found out and it would also be bad for my parents as well.

I had plenty of help in my new home with Jeff, more than enough help. Even though I loved to cook, Jeff told me that's what slaves are for and forbid her from doing it. All our slaves had a frightened look on their face all the time, like they expected anything at any time and they actually jumped when they were called. Once when I sat talking to a couple younger ones, Jeff told me to come to him right away. He took me into another room and said positively not to mix with them. I could see right away that things were mighty different here than at her house on the hill. I didn't want to upset him so I did what he asked.

One night when I asked him why he got so upset with me at the wedding, he said, "I still can't get over you humiliating me by having a slave as an attendant, and worse, your only attendant."

"Well, I thought you'd be over that by now!"

"Over it?" he yelled, "You people over there on the hill think you can get away with your slaves practically living in your house."

I was not about to say just yet that they do. "They're human Jeff, just like you and me."

"No, they are not!"

"Well, you think your way and I'll think mine." He turned and walked away from me.

He really didn't know the slaves lived in the house, but he saw them coming and going from the house. He never got past the sitting room while courting me and everyone pretty much left us to ourselves.

Now Jeff didn't work regular hours, just a few days a week at a store in town selling saddles and horse gear, so he pretty much came and went as he pleased. His brother did absolutely nothing but gamble at night and sleep in the day. Some nights they had to get Jeff to bring him home and other nights he stayed upstairs in the flop house over the saloon. Now that his Dad was gone, he had no one to answer to and so as he got wilder and wilder and spent more and more money. Jeff had too much time on his hands while I taught school. I truly loved what I did, and he became quite jealous. It became harder and harder for me to teach the slaves because he could not find out about that and with no regular schedule it was impossible to know when he would stop in.

CHAPTER 28

Jesse

The place on the hill grew and grew. Dr. Banks and I were spending more time at the clinic and seeing more patients than he ever intended to. Pa, Ma and Mrs. Banks were mostly the ones taking care of the house and farm with Buck and Big John. For a time the Banks were the only white folks up there on the hill, but no one else knew that. The little ones were growing and learning because Lizzy took over teaching them what Cissy had taught her and Noël.

The crops were good, we had rain but finally had to dig a new well and that was expected as we needed more water now. Everybody was making money and we were happy about it. Pa had time to make his furniture and the new tools to make them better. He pretty much had his own little business and Dr. Banks let him keep every penny he made except for ten percent to tithe with on Sunday.

We still gathered every evening to thank the Lord for all He had given us. Pa and Ma always thanked Him for bringing them to Dr. Banks. They still prayed daily for my sister, Esther, and because the Lord said He would, they counted on Him bringing her back to them. She never left their thoughts for a minute.

The only good thing was they knew because the Judge was no longer there that she was probably alright. Plus now with Cissy there, she would tell them if things were bad.

One afternoon Jeff rode by our farm and saw me way out there by the henhouse. He rode up closer and stopped. "Hey, you," he yelled at me. "What are you doing over there?"

"I'm cleaning up my henhouse, why?"

"Your henhouse?"

"Yes."

"Since when do you own anything?"

"Since Dr. Banks said I could. He said, if my Pa built it for me, I could take care of it and he's the boss."

"Oh, I see," he remarked as he rode off to his place.

CHAPTER 29

Cissy

When Jeff arrived home after his talk with Jesse, you could tell he thought the slaves over there were getting a little too big for their britches. They think they're owning things now.

Jeff had begun to ask me for money. I said, "You work and make money plus your Dad left you and Martin lots of money. Why would you need me to give you money?"

This response frustrated Jeff so he shook her, and said, "Don't ask me why I need something. You are my wife and we are supposed to share. Now your Dad has plenty and if he can give so much to his slaves, I would think he would give it to you."

"I wouldn't dream of asking Daddy for money because I have a job and a husband who should take care of me."

"Don't tell me what I should do!"

"Why are you without money after all your Dad left you?"

"Oh, is that why you married me, for money?"

"Oh, for heaven's sake, you know better than that."

"Martin spends and loses every night at the poker table, and he is wasting it all away."

"Well, don't you have your own money and Martin his?"

"He's always asking me for mine and now I am without a cent to my name. We can hardly feed our help, much less pay them anything."

"Jeff, it is not my job to give you money that your own brother is taking from you to play cards with. You could work more at your job and tell Martin he is not going to get any more of your money."

"Cissy, I said, don't tell me what to do and I mean for you to borrow some from your Dad and soon."

"Jeff, I won't do that, not now, not ever."

The look in Jeff's eyes scared me and he looked like he was going to hit me. Instead he pushed me down in a chair and said, "We'll talk about this again and you had better have a different answer." At that he turned and stormed out of the room leaving me shaking.

What has happened to him? He has been different since the day we got married. He's like another person. Oh, my Daddy, could you be right about this marriage? Jeff was real late getting home that night and if he was going to take me to town to school, he would have made me late. Fortunately, it was not a school day but what if it had been; how would she have gotten there? I thought about walking to Mommy and Daddy's house to ask one of them to take her if she had to, but that's a good walk and I would have to leave about an hour earlier to get there. If she did that, then there would plenty of questions which she wasn't ready to answer yet. I know how to ride a horse but not Jeff's and he would be mad that I had left him without his.

I carried on as usual, teaching and coming home, some days Daddy brought me home if he had finished his work at the clinic and Jeff had already gone home from his job. I would sit in the clinic and wait for Daddy on those days, grading papers and planning the next day for my students. I had really rather ride home with Daddy every day as I felt safer but that wasn't really an option.

CHAPTER 30

Dr. Banks

I noticed Cissy's mood change; she was not the happy young girl she used to be and never smiled. There was also a noticeable loss of weight that I could see as the days went on. It was like hugging a skeleton and it gave me the chills, but I didn't pry as Cissy was a grown woman now and she knew we would always be here if she wanted to talk. Still I couldn't shake the feeling things weren't right and it bothered me a great deal. I didn't say anything to Viv for a while, but when Cissy came to visit one Sunday afternoon Viv noticed the weight loss herself and asked Cissy about it. Cissy explained that she was overworked and tired and didn't have time to eat most of the time. Well, she ate with us that day and hardly touched her food even though it was all her favorite dishes.

Viv and I took her aside to ask if there was anything wrong. Cissy had tears in her eyes but said, "no."

"Now Cissy, you can tell us if you are having problems."

"Well, Jeff has changed, he's not the same."

"What do you mean, give us an example."

"Jeff is so demanding all the time. He is jealous of my work or any time I spent away from him or the house even if he isn't there. Jeff is always asking questions about what goes on here at your house. He asked how much money you give your slaves for their work. I told him I didn't know, which is true, but he didn't believe me and got very angry when I wouldn't tell him more."

Then Viv went one step further and asked her about their time alone together. Cissy said, "There is none."

"What do you mean by that?"

"He goes to town all the time and gets in late, so there is no alone time."

She also said she had a hard time awakening him in the mornings to take her to work.

"I will come by and get you and you can ride in with me"

"You don't go in every day."

"But I will, to take you."

"I am afraid if he wakes up and finds me gone, he will be furious."

"So, it has gone that far, that you are afraid of him?"

"Sometimes, yes, Daddy."

"I'm truly sorry about that Cissy, truly sorry."

Now that we were into fall again, it was time to hunt for the winter meat which was deer. Ham and Big John went out and the first day got two on the first shot. That evening they came home and hung the deer from a tree to field-dress which means clean and cut up the meat for cooking. It was also hog killing time and Buck worked hard getting everything cut, cooked, and canned. Jesse made sausage too and what fine breakfasts Violet had for everyone.

We worked hard and ate well thanking God every night for all the provisions he provided. At this evening's prayers, Ham prayed to God to help them have a church of their own. There was one they could go to, but it was way too far. The town's people wouldn't let them have a church real close by and the closest one was probably fifteen miles away.

I said, "Ham, one day you will build your own church. Give it time, God will bless you with a church. But for now, God is right here in this room. Every time we gather, read His book, pray, and ask for His guidance through the Spirit, He is here with us. If we follow Him, He will lead us in the right direction. That's what this book is, His instructional book on how we are to live and worship Him. It also tells us how He will bless us for doing just that. I also want us to pray for my daughter Cissy, as she is going through a rough period right now in her marriage. We ask God to protect her and let no harm come to her. We pray that she will lean on God to help her at this time."

Everyone looked at each other but said not a word. I knew I should answer that look before they drew some conclusion of their own so I responded, "I will say this right now, it seems she has a jealous husband and he is asking too many questions about our life up here. He gets mad when she doesn't tell him what he wants to know. So, I am asking you to be really careful in your comings and goings. Watch your back. Also be sure and carry your gun for protection and know this, that if anything ever happened to any of you, I would go to my grave taking up for you. I would make sure the guilty party was punished and put away. You all mean that much to Vivian and me. And keep in mind If God is for us, who can be against us? And He will settle every dirty, nasty deed that has ever been done, one day."

A few months later after everyone had prayers and were fixing to go to bed, there was a knock on the kitchen door. Since Viv and I had already gone to their room, Ham answered it and was so shocked at what he saw.

CHAPTER 31

Cissy

Ham exclaimed, "Cissy! my goodness child, what has happened to you?" He brought me in the kitchen and sat me down, then told Violet to "Go get Dr. Banks and quick."

When Dr. Banks came to the kitchen and saw her sitting there at the table, he said, " Oh dear Lord, my Cissy!"

I looked up at Daddy and asked, "Why has he changed so?"

"Who darling?"

"Jeffrey, he's so different."

"Has he done this to you, Cissy?"

"He got furious cause he saw me in town today talking to Jesse."

"You were supposed to be careful about things like that."

"Jesse was just loading some books on the wagon for me to store at home. He just happened by and proceeded to help me. Everyone knows he's one of ours."

"Not yours Cissy, he's one of mine and there is a difference now."

"When I got home this afternoon Jeff and Martin were just sitting there like they were waiting for me, and I could tell they had been drinking for a while. I never saw Jeff drink before today. He said he saw me in town and that he was going to teach me a lesson never to speak to a man slave again as long as I lived. He hit me so hard I fell back against the wall and when I got up, he hit me again in the stomach. His brother was sitting there laughing and I couldn't believe what was happening to me. Oh Daddy, I really did love him but he was different before."

"I know sweetheart. He was different because he wanted you, but inside he's always had that same character as his Dad and brother. Now let me check you over and put something on that eye. You will not go back there tonight or most likely ever. When he and his brother sober up tomorrow, he's gonna come and try to take you back, but I'll be here. School is out for the summer so you don't have to go back into town for a while."

"Daddy, I'm scared."

"I know, and you should be, but I will handle this. That boy made me a promise when he asked for your hand in marriage."

CHAPTER 32

Dr. Banks

Ham, Jesse, Big John, Buck and I were waiting the next day when Jeff and his brother rode up like clockwork around noon. Only Jeff came to the door and when I opened it, he said, "Where's my wife?"

"She's in bed and hurt pretty bad."

"I want her home with me."

"What for, so you can hit her again?"

"I didn't hit her hard and she knows I had good reason."

"No man ever has a reason to hit a woman."

"Well, she was out flirting with another man and he was black."

"Flirting you say?"

"Yes, flirting."

"Well, was this the man she was flirting with?" Then Jesse came from behind the door.

"Yeah, that's him."

"He belongs to me and he has known Cissy since they were both little children. He was helping her load books onto the wagon, that's all."

"She knows she's not to talk to slaves, yours, or anybody else's."

"Well, we see things quite different in our house."

"She goes by my rules now, go get her."

"No, she's not coming back there ever again. You made a promise to me when you asked my permission to marry her. Now you have struck her not once but twice in a fit of anger over something you thought you saw. She will stay with me till she heals and then she will decide what she wants to do about the situation."

"I will bring the law out here and get her."

"Bring them then and I will show them what you did to the teacher of their children. And then we will run you scoundrels out of town."

"We'll see about that."

"Yes, we'll see, and the sooner the better. And if you come up here again, I or my men will shoot you on sight and yes, my slaves are allowed to carry a gun."

The two left in a huff and were not heard from for a while, but we all knew anything could happen at any time. All of us men took turns each night keeping watch along with the dogs over the place for a long time.

CHAPTER 33

Big John

A couple of weeks later Cissy rode into town with Mrs. Banks, Lizzy and me. Jeff saw her and Lizzy placed her hand on Cissy's back as reassurance she wasn't alone. Cissy was shaking as she watched Jeff stomp over to the wagon speaking through clenched teeth, "I need to talk to you Cecilia. Alone."

"Anything you have to say, you can say it right here."

"I want you to come home."

"Jeff you have not treated me right since the day we married. You completely changed and you tricked me into believing you were a good man. It was over before it started."

"Well, you did something without telling me."

"And that was?"

"Bringing that slave girl into the church and letting her be a part of our wedding."

"Well, you know Jeff, until I said I do, I didn't have to tell you or ask you anything. And I wouldn't have married a man I thought would want to control everything I thought and did. Now that's not my way of living. I am a free person, who even in marriage will not tolerate being controlled by another person and the one thing I live by is the Bible, where it says, love your neighbor as yourself, not just if he's white like you. So, get back from the wagon, I'll be out soon to get my things."

Cissy explained on the way home she wanted to get her books amongst other things and hoped her Daddy and I would go with her. Mrs. Banks said they needed to wait a while till things simmered down a bit.

A day or two later the maid from the Catron house came to see Dr. Banks as a patient supposedly and actually told him when she knew for sure that the son's wouldn't be there at the house. So, a week later Cissy, Dr. Banks, Buck and I went to the house. When we approached the porch, the maid came running out yelling, "They done burnt your books Miss Cissy!"

"Oh no!" cried Cissy

The maid led us to the pile out back of the house where the fire was still smoldering. "They done that just before they left for town."

"I need those books for school, Daddy!"

"I know Cissy but it's not the end of the world, now let's go and get your clothes and other things." The maid gave us a few food items, jams, jellies, etc. and put the clothes in the wagon while Dr. Banks and Cissy went back for another check to see if they had everything. It was getting dark so Cissy hugged the maid and thanked her for all her help then we all hurried to get home.

Ham came out to help unload the wagon and jumped back when he saw a girl underneath all those clothes. "Pa Pa!"

"Oh Esther, I don't believe it!"

"Pa Pa, oh Pa Pa."

Mrs. Banks and Violet came running out to see what all the commotion was about and when Violet saw her daughter she fell to her knees. "Dear Lord, thank you Lord."

Violet was overcome with emotion. She hugged Esther and ran to the house with her as if to let her know once you are in the house on the hill, nothing will harm you. The hugging and crying with joy went on all day into the night it seemed.

Us men had a strong feeling something would happen that night, call it our God given protective instincts. We didn't know what, but something, so we kept watch all night taking shifts to guard our house and everyone in it. About three o'clock in the morning, we saw a glow coming from the lower field, near the creek and then smoke. "Oh no, the henhouse! Get Jesse!"

Jesse jumped on his horse with a bucket on either side and so did Dr. Banks, Buck, Ham and I. We did what we could but were only able to save a few hens. It was heartbreaking to see all those innocent lives lost for no good reason. The rest was a total loss and Jesse, with tears in his eyes, couldn't believe someone would do that.

Cissy came running and held Jesse in her arms. "Oh Jesse, I am so sorry. It's all my fault."

"No Cissy, we can rebuild, I'm just glad it wasn't our house and those in it."

"He wouldn't!"

"I'm not so sure about that." One things for sure, they will keep watch every night for a long, long time.

CHAPTER 34

Dr. Banks

Cissy approached me the next day and asked, "Where was God while all this was happening?"

"He was right here Cissy and He kept us all safe. He will watch over his children who love and obey Him. Which was more important, the henhouse or getting Esther back? We have prayed and prayed for her return and I'm sure her brother Jesse would give up several henhouses for his sister, don't you?"

"Why did Jeff turn out to be so bad when I thought he was a good man?"

"Because he was not a believer."

"But Daddy, he went to church every Sunday."

"And Cissy, so did his father, the Judge. There are many who go to church to be seen and have all sorts of reasons why they are there, except for the real reason they should be. Let me tell you there are a lot of wolves in sheep's clothing out there. I am sorry it didn't work out for you sweetheart, but next time you will make sure he believes as you do, otherwise it will not work."

"There won't be a next time Daddy."

"Oh yes there will be and God already has him picked out for you. Now let's concentrate on getting you some books ordered."

Within a couple days the whole town had heard about the Catron brothers burning Cissy's precious books and Jesse's henhouse. They took up a collection to buy her books and several men, all white mind you, appeared to help rebuild the henhouse. Whether they knew it was Jesse's or not, no one said a word.

One of the council members told me that the Catron boys had been out gambling and drinking that night of the fire. The council had a pretty good idea the brothers were the ones at fault and said, if there was one more incident out of either of them, they would be run out of town.

"Thank you," I said, "Can you promise me I can buy every slave belonging to the deceased Judge if and when that happens?"

"You have my word on it, Dr. Banks."

We had gotten rid of the first henhouse we built up near the house so now with on a couple of mature chickens who survived, we had to buy eggs again at church on Sunday until Jesse could get started again. Jesse had learned from years of abuse before he came to our place not to show a lot of emotion especially about anything he cared about as it could and would be used against him. After this turn of events he had a look that I never saw on him before. Violet mentioned this to me and I said I would have a talk with him to see if he could draw him out a little.

That evening after prayers, I asked Jesse if he would come outside and take a walk with me. Jesse didn't say a word, he just followed. Sometimes the rhythm of walking in nature with someone you trust is all you need to help get your heart recentered.
Once we were a good bit away from the house, I said "You know

Jesse, we all know this has been a terrible thing for you to cope with and there are lots of reasons why you should be mad or bitter. Number one, because they retaliated towards you and you were only helping your dear friend load books on her wagon. Number two, because of your color. That is completely unfair and unbrotherly. Now Jesse, being the man you are right now; you need to know how God took you from an unbelievable situation to led you and your family to us. As long as I have breath in me, I will not let any harm come to you. That's not to say you won't have problems in the future or after I am gone, but I am with you and for you always."

Jesse was listening but not ready to respond, so I just kept talking.

"He has also enabled you to be taught things that you would have never been taught. Thanks to our Cissy and her love of teaching, regardless of the things that could happen to her if it ever got out, she gave you all the building blocks you need to take your education to the next level. You could choose to go further with your medical training, if you ever really wanted that, but I will not be like my father and push it upon you. That has got to come from something inside you. If you want a better life, I will help you in every way I can so that you will be able to practice medicine one day. And until the day comes when they allow blacks to practice down in these parts, you can treat your own people and farm at the same time, just like I do."

"What about the Catron brothers?"

"There will always be people in this world like the Catron brothers and their father. You have to feel sorry for them and forgive them because those boys didn't have the kind of role model you had as a father. Ham is a good man. They will suffer a lot more from that than you will ever imagine. God has already done much for you and will continue to bless you so don't harbor unforgiveness in your heart. He says we are to forgive like he has forgiven us. So, Jesse, my boy, walk with your head held high because you are a child of God. He will order your steps and you must follow His lead. I know this was not about the henhouse as much as it was a personal thing

HEAVEN ON THE HILL

with you, but you must rise above that and consider what sort of people you were dealing with and don't try to get even because God can handle that so much better than we can, and your conscience will be clear."

"What chance to I have at a different future if every time I start to have success, someone like those men takes it away from me & there isn't a thing I can do about it?

"No one can take your education away from you. You know, Jesse, if you were to take a test today on what you have learned from Cissy, you could probably pass the seventh grade or higher. Now you know not too many white men have gotten that far in school. Like I said, God has blessed you, Jesse. You didn't come to me by accident. And even if by law, you are not free, you know that I would allow you to further your studies in medicine and go as far as you need to go in that field. I consider you free and hope that you feel free, even under the circumstances of the laws in Mississippi. I truly believe that Lincoln will change that law one day real soon. If I weren't afraid some harm would come to you, I would let you go anywhere you wanted alone, but there is such racial prejudice here, that you can't be safe. They could hang you next to the road somewhere and just say they got you mixed up with someone else and not even go to jail for it. That's why I ask you to ride two and two and both carry a gun and try not to ride out at night unless you are with me."

"I know."

"You have let me go on and on but you haven't said very much, Jesse. Are you hearing what I'm saying to you? I'm very proud of you, as proud as if you were my own son and I'm darn sure your Pa Pa feels the same. Remember your people are going to need a doctor after I'm gone. If you are lucky like me, you could have the best of both worlds, egg farmer and a medical practice at the same time. Just don't waste your precious time thinking about what's happened here in the past couple of days cause those guys aren't worth your time."

We walked the rest of the way back home in silence and I just prayed to God that I had chosen the words He needed Jesse to hear in that moment. Only God can change hearts. I must follow God and trust Him with the consequences.

CHAPTER 35

Violet

Cissy was afraid to go anywhere and so afraid to go into town especially to teach in the fall. Mrs. Banks told her most everyone would be watching those Catron boys and Dr. Banks would be in town most days at his clinic. They would ride in together and Big John or Buck could keep watch while she taught. All he would have to do is fire one shot and everyone would come running. Mrs. Banks begged Cissy one morning, "Please don't let it ruin your summer."

Not a word was mentioned anywhere about Esther, our latest runaway. We kept her well-hidden. She was such a beautiful girl and we were so afraid of what would happen to her when they found out she was gone. Esther was also afraid for the maid who hid her in the wagon. But all the maid had to say is that she ran away during the night. Esther told me that the Judge kept her under his control all the time along with a couple others. He brought her to his room on a regular basis. His wife knew all about it and that's what drove her crazy. He didn't seem to care if she knew. If she happened to come to his room and see him with one of the girls, he yelled at her and told her to mind her own business. Esther would hear her crying way into the night and in the daytime he sort of pampered her for the benefit of the boys or the older maids who liked to gossip.

Mrs. Banks was so happy to have Cissy home and I was the happiest I have ever been having my whole family back. I thanked God every day for these blessings and that we all had a wonderful family to work for who treated us like we are somebody, and Mrs. Banks would say, "you are somebody."

The other places we worked fed their hogs better than their workers. Here we got good food and good pay for our labor and all Dr. Banks expects is one tenth of it to go into the church offering. I do wish we had our own church so we could give our tenth to our own instead of those people who won't even let us go inside their church.

Mrs. Banks explained, "I know it seems unfair to you, but you are giving to the Lord, not the people that go there. The Lord says give, it's not up to us to decide what happens to it. You say to yourself; I am giving to God and he will put it where it needs to go and forget it. If you folks want to give us the tithe of ten percent and we then put it in the bank. We will mark it 'Church Fund,' so by the time you get your church built think how much you would have saved for all sorts of things the church will need. Now we will tell everyone on the farm about this fund and even though you don't see this church yet, you just imagine it and know where it's going one day soon. I know Dr. Banks would approve of this as well and I will tell him what you have planned to do."

Cissy told Lizzy she was not too happy to be back home because she felt if she had done things differently Jeff might not have changed so and it felt like she was going backwards in her life instead of forward. But Dr. Banks assured her Jeff's ugly side would have shown itself sooner or later, better sooner and hope she was not already expecting. Cissy exclaimed, "Oh dear, I hadn't even thought of that!"

The men's vegetable garden was flourishing and making money for them and the women were working the one close to the house. We put up enough food each summer to survive for two years or so in case our crops failed for some reason, like too much rain or too little.

Ham's baby was his cotton. Oh my, was he ever proud of that and he should be as it sold really well. Jesse's egg business was off and running again, but he Buck with him whenever he went out to check on the hens since it was away from the house. We were always on our guard and ready for anything.

Cissy started back teaching again and if anyone saw the likes of Jeff or his brother Martin, they lit out for the clinic to tell the doctor. That summer Dr. Banks thought it would be best if Cissy learned how to use a gun. It was something he never even thought about until this episode with Jeff, so he showed her how to load, shoot and clean the shotgun so it wouldn't stick when she needed it most. The shotgun was the best gun option for her as she could aim anywhere in the general direction of someone wanting to hurt her or the kids and stop them without having to be as precise as a she would need to be with a pistol or rifle. She kept it with her anytime she was in town.

Ham had made her a big stick with a hook on it so Cissy could hang the shotgun up high where the kids couldn't reach it but could get it down in a hurry if needed. Ham had all kinds of things he could make and use in the event of an emergency. He truly was amazing and I was proud he was my husband. All these preparations were for the safety of the children as well. If it weren't for the children, she could keep the shotgun under her desk since it had to be loaded and ready to shoot.

Cissy was a good teacher and they all loved her. As usual in the evenings and on Saturdays she taught the younger ones including my little grandbaby Nathaniel. Some of the older ones who wanted to learn to spell and write their name would join in too. Believe it or not little Noël could even help them teach us too as she started very young and was smart as a whip. Esther was also eager to learn because Lizzy, her little sister, knew so much more than she and you know how competitive siblings can be. It pleased Esther when Cissy said, "Don't worry you will catch up, we will work over time with you to be sure of it."

CHAPTER 36

Dr. Banks

The Catron brothers hadn't been seen in church since their father died, but they were seen at night in town playing poker. We heard with nobody working, the money left for them by the Judge was quickly running out and they really couldn't afford the number of slaves they had. One of the council members told me that two men and two women slaves would be up on the block for sale on Saturday. So, I asked the council member if he would bid on them and buy them for me as I didn't want to create any more trouble with that family.

So that Saturday Ham, Buck and I went to town. When bidding time came I asked Ham and Buck if any of these looked familiar. I for sure wanted to get the young women away from the place and the men too, but one of the men looked pretty old. Ham said, "I don't know either of these fellas and you ain't gonna get much work out of either of 'em. One be way too old and the other has a bad leg. That's why he's selling 'em. Can't afford to feed 'em & ain't making much money off 'em."

When I got up close and saw the condition of the men I went over to the councilman to ask him bid for me but only slightly higher each time so as not to lose the bid. The councilman bought the two men and pretended to take them out back to put them in his wagon but covered them up in mine instead and told them to lay low for safety. The councilman came back and bid on the two women, one older and one around twenty-five or so. He purchased them and did the same thing with them as the men. Ham rode up front with me and Buck in the back with the new slaves until we were way out from town and then he partially uncovered them till they got home so it would be more comfortable for them but they could still hide if needed.

The women were waiting with a cool dipper of water and sat them down inside the porch to unchain them. Lizzy and Esther ran to close the shutters on the porch side of the house to create a little extra privacy in case someone unexpected came riding up. We all talked and made sure everyone was fed. I could tell they couldn't understand why they were bought by the councilman and then brought here so I explained who we are and of course they knew Lizzy and Esther. The younger one called Isaiah said to Esther, "So this where you ran off to?"

The older one noticed everyone smiling and at ease. He asked me, "Why you be buying an old folk like me who can't do you no good?"

"Well, first of all you are not that old and I will not work you on jobs that are for younger men. There will be plenty of things for you to do here. Now who all else is out there at the Catron place?"

"The old cook Bertha and one maid."

"I think I have met her."

"And two other men younger than us that work the fields. Those two brothers ain't doin nothing but sleeping all day and staying out all night. Some nights they come home happy cause they won some money, but other nights they just fall asleep soon as they get home, drunk and mad cause they lost. Most times they lose."

"What ever happened to the overseer out there?"

"Oh, he left when the boys couldn't pay him his full pay, most times they couldn't pay at all. We couldn't go nowhere cause those boys so mean they would hunt us down and shoot us or hang us one."

"Could they afford to keep the other four?"

"No sa, not when they lose more than they win. Now if they can feed the others they'll stay on, what more can they do, they can't just up and walk."

"Well now, Ham and Jesse will show you to the room you'll be sleeping in and see what all you brought with you in case any of it needs to go in the cellar to keep it fresh. Cissy and Lizzy will show the women where they'll be sleeping as well."

"You mean we stay in the same house as you?"

"Yes, that's right, we have plenty of rooms in this house. Now all I ask is you don't venture too close to the main road since the brothers use that road as well. You also can not go into town without me, Mrs. Banks or Cissy being with you and you'll be in disguise, for fear someone will tell the brothers. Never ride out alone for any reason. Ham will tell you all you need to know about safety. We have several places to hide in the house and a cellar for keeping food cold, but also a hideaway down there as. The main thing now is to keep you safe as the brothers would get mighty angry if they found out I bought you. When the women go outside, don't everyone go at once because we don't want folks to know how many live up here on the hill."

CHAPTER 37

Vivian

The first night with our four new house members, they all looked as puzzled as everyone else did at first sitting at our huge table in the kitchen with big bowls of corn, potatoes, fried chicken and gravy plus the two big baskets of biscuits that were passed around. Ham said grace and then told them to dig in. There were smiles all around the table. And the peach pies topped off the supper that evening. Afterwards we all stepped outside on the side porch as it was still warm in the evenings and got to know each other better.

After a little bit Morgan motioned for me to come join him alone in the yard looked at me and asked, "Are you happy, Viv?"

"Yes, Morgan I truly am even though I am beginning to feel a little outnumbered about now."

He laughed and said, "Sweetheart I have plans for that real soon."

"Really, like what?"

"I haven't thought it all out yet, but God has placed something on my heart to do with this land and all these hardworking people, he has given us. He has blessed our lives so much and we must be good stewards of what has been entrusted to us. But I need to know if you still want to stand with me in these wild dreams of mine?"

"I'm happy when you're happy, you know that."

"What a wonderful woman you are Vivian. I am so lucky to have you. I never intended to get this involved with so many slaves, but these people have such a need for love and respect with a hunger for freedom and contentment. They have lived in fear too long. Now let's get back in and take them to the sitting room."

Everyone gathered around sitting here and there. After getting a few more chairs from the kitchen, Morgan read from his worn Bible and Ham's was open too as he listened with the others. Then as always, Morgan asked everyone to kneel in front of their chairs while they prayed. This time Ham thanked God for bringing all his family together, which he thought would never happen in a million years. Morgan thanked God for bringing these new people into our home and how blessed he felt to be able to obtain them and let them know of freedom for the first time in their lives.

Ham found out the older man, Tom, was a beekeeper. Tom knew all about bees and making honey, so Ham planned to him get that started in a couple of days. They were going to set up the hives down by the berry patch on the way to the creek as it would be good for the berry crop and good for the honey. Ham talking as much to himself as any of us said, "Wouldn't that be good having our own honey to go on those biscuits in the mornings and also to sell in town or at church?"

Now he was thinking like Morgan, everything could be a money maker.

CHAPTER 38

Isaiah

None of us could believe what was happening to us. It felt like God had worked a miracle in our lives. We had only seen the house on the hill from the road to the Catron house and thought what a beautiful place. Now we were truly aware of the beauty of the inside of this home and the people who lived here.

Dr. Banks had told us the night before that our freedom would mean many obstacles we would have to face, like always being on guard, always moving in groups, sometimes changing our looks when going into town, and never gathering on the grounds around the house in groups especially not the women.

He said, "We want people to think we have a normal number of slaves, especially kitchen help. Field hands are different. Some people have as many or more than twenty on a large farm such as ours. Now everyone knows while I'm away or in town at the clinic, Ham is in charge of the farm and all slaves. The councilmen wish I had a white man as overseer, but I told them I could not find one I trusted like I do Ham. We also have a couple signals. My wife has a beautiful voice and can sing like a bird, very high. She will start singing the song 'Nobody Knows the Troubles I've Seen' and you can hear her all over this farm. When you hear her sing that song, that's your signal to get away from what you're doing and take cover, until the trouble is gone. If you hear Ham shoot once in the air, you will know there is bad trouble and wait for Ham to tell you what to do. He will pass instructions to you from one man to another. Once the coast is clear and no need to worry anymore, Vivian will sing 'Victory in Jesus' so you can continue what you were doing."

We were told that two men would take turns every night, four hours each, keeping watch over this place and the people inside. We never let their guard down and it seemed the two dogs on the place knew their job as well.

CHAPTER 39

Vivian

After a few months we could all tell that Esther and Isaiah were more than a little interested in each other. The light in their eyes was something to see and who wouldn't want to be Esther, she was the prettiest dark-skinned woman I ever saw. Ham was all right with the match, but Violet wanted Esther to herself for a while longer. It seemed Esther had been here such a short time and Violet had missed her so badly all those years.

But as time went on, Violet came around, and knew Esther's happiness was so important especially with what she had been through. Isaiah didn't care and he wanted her anyway regardless of her past. "Her past wasn't her fault and she looks past my scars as well as I see past hers," he said.

There were plenty of jobs to do around the house. If it was summer the older folks and Isaiah would sit on the porch to shell peas, string beans, shuck corn, peel peaches, water the flowers, feed the hogs or any number of other chores which they loved doing all those things. It felt good to be able to contribute to the house without trying to force a body to do what it could no longer do. During the fall there were nuts to gather and crack, apples to peel, canning of apple butter, sewing of quilts, sheets and pillowcases. The old men still liked to cut and split wood for the big fireplace plus several on the upper floors as we couldn't all fit in one room on the cold nights anymore.

There never was a dull moment. Morgan even used a little of the "found" money and bought a spinning wheel, to the delight of all the women, me included.

CHAPTER 40

Dr. Banks

One evening Jesse came and told me, "I have thought about our conversation many months ago and have decided to try doctoring. I realize black folks will need a doctor to treat them. So far you have been willing to treat them where none of the others would. If you would continue to school me and teach me as much as it would take to pass the written exam, I am willing to learn."

I have never been so happy; I hugged Jesse and danced around like we were partners at the barn dance. It was the first time I had ever heard Jesse really laugh. We ran into the house to tell Ham and Violet. They were so happy they cried. Jesse said, "Now wait till I see if I can pass the tests for heaven's sake!"

From that day on for the next year Jesse and I studied together. I took him to the clinic and showed him every old instrument and the newest ones too. Jesse delivered several babies on his own with me showing him all about the complications, but I clarified, "most of the time nature does it all."

Jesse dressed every wound and I let him diagnose illnesses. I had given him an old book of symptoms and let him use it when he was unsure of a diagnosis. If he still wasn't sure, we would talk it over and I would ask him what he thought, and nine out of ten times Jesse was right. I explained, "The more people you see the easier that gets. Unless it's obvious what's wrong you rule out things, one after another till you narrow it down to this or that."

Once in a while we would have a death of a person brought in from the countryside and no one knew them. In that case I would open him up to let Jesse see all the internal organs and see if we could figure out what he had died of. Jesse never flinched. He was cool as could be and actually liked that part as he found it easier to learn that way than from pictures in a book. It was truly hard work, but Jesse was a good student.

One night after a particularly long day at the clinic, Jesse told me, "I never ever thought I could do anything like this, being just a dumb slave boy."

Dr. Banks said, "Jesse your brain is as good as my brain, but God Himself brought us together for a reason and that's where the opportunity comes in. Someone was interested in you enough and cared enough about you to help you develop that good brain of yours. God, not I, has done all this for you because He loves you. You walk the straight and narrow path with Him and He will bless all your days."

Long after the sun set that day, two men approached the house. Buck was on watch that night and called out while the dogs were right on them. I pulled on my pants and walked outside. "What's the problem out here?"

"We come to fetch you Dr. Banks, there's been a bad accident in town. One of the Catron brothers has burnt hisself real bad."

"Ok, I'll get my bag. Jesse, saddle up my horse as fast as you can."

There wasn't time to saddle two horses, so Jesse and I rode together as fast as old George could run. When we entered the saloon there was Jeff lying on the floor.

"Tell me what happened here?" I asked as I opened my bag.

"Well, he was sitting here playing cards and all of a sudden we saw his shirt on fire. Seems some ashes from his cigar fell on his shirt and the thing just caught fire. He was thrashing about so much we couldn't get it off him. Looks like he's burnt pretty bad."

"Yes, it looks that way. Jesse and a couple of you guys help carry him over to the clinic; I have more equipment over there."

I doctored stayed with him all night and so did Jesse. A large crowd had gathered outside that evening, waiting to see if he made it or not. His brother sat in the waiting room in the clinic anxious for any news. Martin had sobered up by then and knew what was happening.

About eleven in the morning I went out and got Martin and told him to step inside. "I'm sorry son, he was burnt from his waist up and there was not much we could do but keep him from so much pain. I am sorry for your loss and now there is no one left but you, Martin, my boy. Let this be a lesson to you tonight, if you continue doing what you're doing and living like you do, you will end up just like your brother here." I wanted to say like your Dad too but held that part back. "So, I suggest right now you get down on your knees and ask God to change you."

"What a sad night," I told the people outside. "Such a young man and things could have been so different." Jesse and I took the body back to his house for the maids to clean and prepare. His brother was in bad shape and all alone now. What would become of him? Only time will tell. I didn't see patients that day, I was totally exhausted.

Cissy cried and cried and said between sobs, "Oh Daddy, I did love him." She was taking all this pretty bad which was understandable.

"I know my girl." Now there was another Catron laid to rest.

CHAPTER 41

Cissy

I was still very sad. I am a widow now and still felt if I hadn't had Lizzy in my wedding, that maybe things would have been different. Mommy said, "But you love Lizzy, and you know how happy you made her by being in your wedding. Jeff was prejudiced and he was raised that way. You couldn't have changed that, and you wouldn't have liked to live that way. Don't look back Cissy, instead look ahead to make a difference in someone else's life now and God will put some excitement in your life. You are still very young and have many joys ahead of you."

At least now I didn't have to worry about Jeff bothering me or the kids at school and I could focus on my teaching. I would now be safe in town and it was time to get ready for another barn dance. Oh, the cooking and the sewing of new clothes! Whatever would we do if we didn't have the dance to look forward to?

Esther and Isaiah were so in love, and everyone said a marriage was due to happen soon. Daddy said, "We wish we had a preacher to make it legal, but we do with what we have. Now we all know that when two or more, who love God, are gathered together in His presence and your vows are said before Him to be witnessed before your fellow believers, you are truly considered married in His eyes.

So let us have a wedding and join this loving couple together so that they may be fruitful and multiply."

And everybody said "Amen," to that. There was a celebration of all celebrations at the house on the hill. Food and dancing in the main hall. Daddy made a toast and everyone cried for a few minutes but shortly there was laughter again, with Ham playing the harmonica and the wedding couple danced together by themselves.

What a handsome couple they made and the look of happiness on their faces was beautiful. Esther had come from a house of torture to a home on the hill that was full of love and nobody to ever judge her for her past. The fun lasted till almost midnight, and everyone was ready to call it a day especially the bride and groom.

The barn dance was not far off now and I wanted a store-bought dress this time. I told Mommy that I loved the dresses she and Violet made for me, but I am a very grown woman now and making my own money so I could afford one. Of course, Mommy understood and said, "I will go with you into town and help you pick out a beautiful dress."

"No, Mommy, I saw one in a catalog that I just love and besides if I buy one in the only dress shop in town I am sure someone else will have the exact same dress on that night."

"You could be right, Cissy, but it might take a couple weeks to get here."

"That's okay, we have time as I ordered the dress several weeks ago and it's due to arrive any day now."

I would never want to upset my mother in any way as I loved her too much, but I really wanted to look special this time for many different reasons. Some of the women my age in town were calling me some unattractive names having to do with being a schoolteacher, widowed, strict and all those things they say about a schoolteacher. Soon they would be calling me an ole spinster. Now I knew that was to be expected when you were a teacher, but the fact that the children loved me so and I was making a difference was all that mattered. They could say what they wanted, but I just wanted to look really special for this dance.

Sure enough, my dress arrived in time and it truly was lovely. It fit me perfectly almost like it was made for me and I knew without a doubt, no one would have one like it. When you are married to a man that treated you badly or hit you, that got around town and they all looked at you differently somehow. Almost like you provoked him or any number of other little secrets that they conjured up in their minds. Since that happened to me, I have felt like everyone watched me wherever I went and were whispering behind my back.

CHAPTER 42

Dr. Banks

There were several new families at this dance. Cissy was again the hit of the evening. In her pale pink dress with her black hair tied up in back with a matching pink ribbon, no one could take their eyes off her. Even the older men there were watching every move she made and the wives were absolutely disgusted with their husbands. But her beauty was so outstanding it was hard not to watch her move across the floor. She met two new fellows there and danced twice with one and three times with the other, along with the regular guys who were always there. Viv and I noticed that she seemed happy again and after all she had been through, that was good for a change.

Standing back from the crowd, you could catch a look now and then or a conversation in front of you when they thought you couldn't hear. One young lady there who had also danced with the new fellows was saying something about Cissy; couldn't catch it all but something like she shouldn't be at the dance, she should still be in mourning for her late husband. I wanted to say something so bad but kept my thoughts to myself. It was eight months ago that Jeff had died and besides, they were separated because of his ill treatment of her and in my opinion, she shouldn't be in mourning at all after the way he abused her. Viv heard her too and I had to hold her back when she started to say something.

"All I wanted to do was let them know we were her parents and heard what she said."

"Yes, but the dance is a happy time for everyone and we don't want to stir up any trouble."

It's really hard for a parent not to take up for their children especially when you know the circumstances. Going home Cissy mentioned that one of the new fellows was going to preach next Sunday. I said, "What?"

"Our pastor is getting ready to retire around the first of the year and they are listening to new preachers to see who they would like to replace him."

"Why hadn't we heard that news before?"

"Well, we have missed the last two Sundays because you were out on a case, and I was sick with that horrible cold the next Sunday," said Viv.

"Oh that's right. I forgot about that, Viv. He didn't look old enough to be a preacher."

"Honey, that's because all our preachers have been white haired as far back as I can remember."

"Mommy, when he told me he was thirty, I almost fell over, he didn't look near that old!"

"Well how old do you feel, Cissy?"

"I really haven't thought about it all that much."

"You're not that much younger than he is."

"Well, he sure was nice."

"And the other fellow?"

"Both were really nice, but the preacher was nicer."

"Let's hope they're not brothers!" Viv exclaimed as I rolled my eyes.

"No, they're from different families and his name is Jeremiah, and his sister's name is Sadie, who I also met tonight."

"What's his last name?"

"Woodley."

"Well now let's see, how does Jeremiah and Cecilia Woodley sound Cissy?"

"Oh, Daddy, don't do that."

"What?"

"Make something out of nothing."

"Just teasing sweetheart."

Viv punched me in the ribs. "Yeah, another wedding, that's really what we need around here."

"What we need," I teased, "are some grandchildren around here, Vivvy."

"Morgan stop it, you're embarrassing Cissy now."

"Oh alright."

"Anyway, I have enough children to take care of at school Daddy."

"Alright darlin, whatever you say."

"Thank goodness we were home now and we can talk about something else." Viv said as she changed the subject.

Over the next couple of days Cissy told Viv she did think Jeremiah was quite nice and much too handsome a man to be a preacher, that black hair as black as mine and tall, well over six feet. She told Viv the morning after the dance that it was the first time in a long time, she had sweet dreams that night. And for some strange reason, she was still thinking about him all the next day as well.

Now Ham and I hadn't talked much lately because all my time was spent going to the clinic and teaching Jesse all I could. I hardly had time anymore to work in the fields like I loved or with the livestock, which I also loved. But one evening after supper I sat down with Ham on the porch and we began to talk about what to do with the land down near the creek that's not being used. "I don't rightly know Dr. Banks, but have you heard some of ole Catron's land is gonna be up for sale soon?"

"No, when did you hear that?"

"Other night at the barn dance, some of his men told me Martin's having a rough go of it and needs some money really bad so he's fixin to sell part of his land to meet his bills or he'll have to let all his help go."

"Well, I'd rather buy his people than his land."

"Oh, would they be pleased to come up here!"

"Well Ham, we shall see what kind of a deal we can get out of him. If he's having that much trouble he might say yes to anything about now. He just has two women and two men, right?"

"Yes sa, that be about right."

So next morning I rode out to the Catron place which joins our land about a mile up the road. Funny thing a young girl came to the door and when I asked for Martin, she said, "He's still asleep, but I can wake him up."

Well, it was close to noon so, I said, "alright I'll wait." About ten minutes later here he came looking like he had spent the night with the hogs.

"Have a cup of coffee, Dr. Banks?"

"No thank you, I'm here on business Martin."

"What sort of business?"

"I heard you were close to selling part of your land?"

"You interested?"

"Well not exactly, I'm more interested in buying your help."

"My help?"

"I have a lot going on at my place and need a couple good men and my overseer says your men are good workers."

"Well, I wasn't thinking 'bout selling them. If I rent my land out to other people for grazing and tobacco, etc., I won't need the two men cause those people will bring their own help. That might not be a bad idea. How much you willing to pay?"

Morgan told him what he thought they were worth but being now close to fifty-five years of age, he could give him a better deal if he let him have all his help. "You mean the maids too? Well, I'll have to think about that. That's a fair amount of money, but I still need to think on it a while."

"Fine, I'll be back tomorrow morning to see what you've decided. Good day to you Martin." and I rode off. When I got home, Viv asked me how it went and I responded, "I gave him an offer he can't refuse."

"Now that would mean two more here in the kitchen and you know I don't need any more help in here Morgan. Soon we're going to have to do what you planned many years ago. Cissy is bound to find herself a nice husband and sooner or later I'll be the only one around here during the day supervising all these folks and you are not getting any younger either. Besides you and I, there are ten now and if these come there will be fourteen and sixteen counting us. Anymore and they'll start arguing and fighting."

"Why do you say that?"

'That's just life Morgan."

"And Ham and Violet are slowing down some now too. I don't mean they're not doing their fair share of work, but age is creeping up on them just like it is on us."

"Well, I won't jump to any conclusions till I see if Martin will let these four go. And I couldn't leave just one behind, I wouldn't wish that on anyone."

Reading the bible and prayers were at nine that night and someone started singing again which led to several songs and one by one they began to walk to their rooms for the night. Isaiah and Esther arm in arm, said this was something they had dreamed about as youngsters. A real home where you feel wanted and loved. Isaiah said, "I tell you Esther, this is heaven" and she squeezed his hand tightly.

The next day I didn't have to go to Martin's. He was on our porch at nine o'clock in the morning. "Dr. Banks, I feel you have presented a fair deal and because I have me this girl now, I won't be needing a cook or a maid, so you can have 'em all. Could I interest you in some land too in the deal?"

"Martin I would be interested in the land that joins mine at the creek and over. It's I would say about fifty acres or so and I'll give you the best deal I can for the acreage and four slaves. I'll meet you at the bank to settle up in the morning."

"You got a deal, Dr. Banks. I'll meet you there when the bank opens tomorrow."

"Viv, I've never seen a happier face in my entire life. He didn't even have to put his property on the market or wait but two days for his money. I actually believe he would have given me his slaves for nothing, but I was fair and gave him a darn good deal. So now we had four more people to show our way of life and how we treated one another."

CHAPTER 43

Violet

The next day once the sale was done and the four new folks joined our group the old cook, Charlotte, was the happiest one of all. "I done my time there in that prison and now I be free."

"You certainly are now," I said and hugged her to welcome her into our home.

That afternoon two bushels of peaches were put in a big tub of water and each woman got a knife, pan and formed a circle out under the two old pecan trees to peel all two bushels. We sliced them in quarters then put them in the jars for canning we had ready to go. We saved just enough for a couple of peach cobblers that evening and several jars of preserves as well. Us ladies all loved doing this as this was our time to talk and sing some of our favorite songs and now with Charlotte here Mrs. Banks wasn't the only one now who had a talent for singing.

We gave the older folks simple jobs that they could sit and do on the porch. Watering the garden, drawing up the water and shelling nuts, things like that. They had worked so hard in their younger years and welcomed the easier work. The older men could fix most anything and rest when they needed to.

Charlotte said to me one night, "At first we couldn't believe our mealtime with grace, good food and prayers at night, thanking God for bringing us here when it was Dr. Banks who bought us. We thought he had a funny way of thinking, but now we are starting to understand what he be talking about. The Banks truly seemed to believe they were blessed that God had enabled them to purchase us folks and give them a better life after all we had been through."

She said things had gotten some better for them after the overseer left, but the living conditions hadn't changed and the food was awful since the garden hadn't been tended to. Martin Catron was more concerned with his own needs and women now than trying to pay his people and his bills were too much for him.

Even though Charlotte knew a lot about our house on the hill & the kindness of Dr. Morgan since she had been treated by him, Ruby, the younger one, just couldn't get used to white folks treating her so kind. In the beginning she cried a lot and Charlotte, Esther, and Lizzy would sit with her and comfort her as they knew better than anyone the pain in her heart that was trying to heal. Ruby had also been through a lot with old Judge Catron. "I know he be in hell now," said Ruby.

Charlotte said, "Well, we be better off not to even think about somebody we don't have to worry 'bout no more."

"But the nightmares keeps coming back."

"I know, Ruby, but you're safe now, as safe as you will ever be and free. We be free up here in this house and you don't even have to work when you're sick like before."

CHAPTER 44

Ham

The younger women were trying hard to learn to read and write. My Lizzy taught her big sister Esther, Peaches and Ruby in her spare time so they would have a jump start on weekends when Cissy taught them new things. Reading and writing were a must. All this gave me hope that life could be different for my youngins than it had been for me.

Besides the people always asking questions about us folks on the hill and where we were living, things were starting to settle down. We were getting somewhat crowded around the big table in the kitchen. Mrs. Banks suggested we could make a dining room out of one of the huge rooms on the second floor where the main entrance to the home was and I could make a table to seat at least fourteen plus I could fit an extension on to the one we have now. Violet said the dining room was too far to take the food. Mrs. Banks asked, "Well what did the people do who lived here before us?"

"They probably didn't use the big rooms upstairs for that either, Mrs. Banks."

"The way I figure it they used our sitting room as the dining room. Probably never filled all those rooms like we have on all the floors."

The problem with the third-floor rooms was the heat in the summer. Those rooms were so close to the roof and no insulation up there either. Right now, Mrs. Banks, Violet and Cissy used them for a sewing room, a teaching room with lots of books and supplies, a study and stock room for Dr. Banks to keep past records and things like that in. And even with all that, there were still a couple of unused bedrooms up there.

Dr. Banks took me aside and said, "I have an idea. Between you and me, I've been planning for years to section off land down near the creek and henhouse to give each family a piece of land for them to build a house on. You could even build your own church and after a while, another barn."

My eyes got so big and I couldn't hide my smile that reached from ear to ear. 'Oh, that would be mighty nice, Dr. Banks. We could have a house up in no time."

"Yes, Ham, but I don't mean just any ole house, I mean something real nice. And add that fifty acres I just purchased from Martin Catron and that will give us extra land down there too. Now people won't understand how you're able to afford a nice house, but you can tell them to ask me if they have any questions and that you just do what I tell you to do. We will divide the land, so each family gets the same and your tithing money will build a fine church and later can double as a school, but we would have to keep that a secret."

"I am amazed at all this and how generous you are being towards us."

"The way I figured it there will be at least six homes and maybe more. We can still keep the older folks up here with us so we can tend to their needs. But in the end, you will have your own little community and by that time with the new laws you should be entirely free. And who knows, maybe Martin will sell us more land to farm cause I just know he will one day need more money if he doesn't straighten up. Now you and Violet can always stay with Vivian and me for as long as you want to or you can build your own house. That's completely up to you two. We won't feel bad if you decide to have your own place; you sure have earned it and then some. But in the meantime we can start the first new home any time we get the land marked off and the supplies brought in. People in town will ask a lot of questions when you start buying all these supplies but like I said, refer them to me, that you just come to town with a list of what Dr. Banks wants."

Violet and I talked well into the night about all the things that were brought up today with my discussion with Dr. Banks. Violet couldn't make up her mind if she wanted to have a house of her own or stay up on the hill. This had been her home now for many years and she loved it here and she loved Vivian, Dr. Banks and Cissy too, very much. The house would be nice but what would they do with fifty acres of land now that we were slowing down. We didn't want to depend on Jesse all through our old age, especially when one of these days soon he would become a very busy man doctoring and tending his egg farm too. Oh my, what to do, what to do?

CHAPTER 45

Cissy

Sunday the church was packed. The young preacher that I met at the dance was there to preach today. He sat with his sister Sadie who came with him to Winona. We sang two hymns and Mommy sounded even better with the piano, on her solo. Our minister introduced Jeremiah Woodley to the people and he got up and said hello to everyone and then began his sermon, based on the misconception of "good works", getting you into Heaven. Psalm 53:3 says "There are none that do good, no, not even one and nothing we do ourselves gets us into Heaven."

It was a powerful sermon and he had everyone's attention, for sure. He amazed me and I think just about everyone there. After the service everyone crowded around the young preacher and I stood by Daddy outside who wanted to speak to him, I know, but he couldn't get away.

We had a pretty good idea he would be asked to return and be our new pastor. He was truly a remarkable young man. When he saw that we were about to leave, he threw up his hand to wave. He had been invited to lunch with our present pastor after church service and we couldn't stay any longer and then make him late for lunch.

On the way home I said, "Daddy do you think they will ask him to be our new pastor?"

"Don't rightly know, but he sure would get my vote."

"Mine too."

Mommy said, "He is far better than the pastor we have now, and I believe we need someone for our younger members now."

I felt warm all over, like a schoolgirl and thought to myself, "what is wrong with me?" Again, I had sweet dreams that night and prayed that God would let him be their pastor. I knew one thing, I would be in church every Sunday, that's for sure. That thought made me laugh because we had not missed a Sunday since they moved here, except when the snow was too deep or someone was sick.

CHAPTER 46

Jesse

Everyone in town had been asking about the buildings going up on our place. Dr. Banks told me he didn't know what to tell them without lying so he just said, "We are building a couple houses for our slaves, now that we had several, their quarters had become cramped." That satisfied them for a while until the houses really took shape. These homes were far superior to any slave dwelling in these parts or anywhere else for that matter. Certainly, finer than a lot of white folks had which led to some jealousy from the townspeople.

The council had approached Dr. Banks one day as we were leaving the clinic. "Dr. Banks, are you really going to let those darkies live in those nice homes being built out there on your place?"

"I have always paid my slaves a fare wage and given them room for their own garden. If they have the money now to build a fairly nice home out there, it would suit me better to see something nice rather than to see a bunch of shanties on my property. It's their money and my land, so good day gentleman."

CHAPTER 47

Ham

After dinner that evening, we all gathered in the sitting room which was customary right after dinner. Dr. Banks asked me how the buildings were coming along and if we had decided amongst ourselves who should live in the first house.

"If you have any disagreements we will discuss it later, but I want you to get used to having your own sort of council and decide or vote on issues of this nature when you think something is unfair. If someone wants to branch out or move on, talk it out, but just remember if you leave you are on your own."

"Yes, Dr. Banks we have been talking about that. We have been teaching the new folks that they may be free here on this farm, but away from here someone will shoot or hang them if they are caught."

"You are right about that, Ham. I never would try to tie you down and as far as I'm concerned you have been free since the day I brought you here, but only in our own little world up here on the hill. Remember the dangers of trying to break free from the south to go up north. Most of you will have enough money to do just that, but I care about you and want you to live as long as you can."

"Even when we are free, it won't be easy to leave for most of us, but you have given us a chance to save and see how it feels to have something of our own. We have bought our own horses, tools, wagons and lots more.

"Until the law changes you and you are truly free, you will only be safe if you say you belong to me and there will be times that even then, you will be in danger. You know how it feels to have money in your packet and if you left before you become free, by law, you will find it almost impossible to find work anywhere around here, and your money will run out after a while. Now I have a plan for you folks but can't reveal that plan just yet. If you stay, in a few years, down the road, you will be glad you did."

The first house was almost up. We had discussed and voted on who should live in the first one. Since Lizzy and Buck had married the year before and now had a baby on the way plus Nathaniel, and the others had no children yet they decided that they should be the first to have a house of their own. Another month or so and it would be ready to live in.

Violet and I wanted to live with the Banks for as long as they needed them and we were all about the same age anyway and got along better than family. Our youngest daughter Noël would also live with us until she decided to marry. Now these homes would be scattered about, not like the row cabins the slaves had been used to before they came to live with the Banks. We could place them anywhere we chose on our fifty acres of land. Everyone was so excited about having their own land, house and someday a barn with a church. Never would we have thought this possible and who in their right mind would ever want to leave?

And the fact that nearly all of the younger ones could now read and write, at least enough to get by. It was a new world now they could read a newspaper or our Bible. Some of us could even count, add, and subtract, that way we would know if someone was cheating us when we went to market with our tobacco and cotton or what have you. That was so important, and we were proud of the fact. Now we had to be very careful when we caught anyone with a mistake and that's why Dr. Banks would often go with us to market, but we were quick to see a mistake and tell him. Dr. Banks often told them, life will not stand still, nothing stays the same, and one day we would use this knowledge and not be whipped for it. And you could be sure that us folks would be a minority when it came to the knowledge we have.

CHAPTER 48

Dr. Banks

I had been writing to a doctor friend I know in Biloxi called Dr. Horner to see if there was a way to test Jesse without him going up north. Dr. Horner said, "If you send him to me, I will test him." I knew he could pass every aspect of the test because I had tested him over and over again with questions from my exams of twenty years ago. Since I had kept up with the current methods and medications, I had been able to teach Jesse those techniques too. But I knew I still needed to find a way to get him a degree or some kind or papers stating he was capable and had all the necessary requirements to practice. Dr. Horner said, "Send him on. He has had all the hands-on education you can give." All I have to do now is get him to Biloxi. I have an idea, but will have to ask Jesse about this first.

Dr. Horner and I had been in touch by letter several times trying to set a date for Jesse to come there and take the test that would certify him as a doctor. My friend would sit with Jesse while he took the test and sign the papers stating that he had five years of hands-on knowledge which I would also sign saying I had instructed him for that time. Now all we needed was a date to send Jesse to Dr. Horner to take the test. The only thing I hadn't disclosed was the fact that Jesse was a black slave from Mississippi.

Now Jesse needed someone with him on this trip to insure his safety, but I didn't want to leave my family alone or patients without care for that length of time so Cissy said she would go with him by train. She would explain that he was her slave and traveling with her to ensure her safety on this trip. All Jesse had to do was act the part. They pretended the trip had to do with her school work and new books, etc.

The night before their trip, after dinner we sat as we read the Bible and prayed for their safety. We also prayed Jesse would pass the difficult exams. Jesse, being a man of few words, was as calm as could be. When they got there, she would pretend she was seeing her father's friend and wait in another room while he took his tests.

CHAPTER 49

Jesse

Cissy and I thought we would get the stares from people wondering about a white woman and a black male companion, but all Cissy had to do was tell one person why I was with her, and the word would travel fast. Dr. Banks had loaned me some nicer clothes to wear but not a suit, thinking that might look a little strange for a slave.

We had more serious matters on our minds and Cissy tutored me all the way to Biloxi on the difficult spelling and medical terms. Thank goodness we had a private cabin so no one could overhear us and ask questions. We were both excited about our first train ride, but Cissy thought it so strange that I didn't seem the slightest bit worried about the tests.

When we arrived, no one seemed to care if Cissy was accompanied by me. I guess in a place this size, you see everything.

The test took nearly all day the first day and five hours of the second day. Dr. Horner let me sleep in his office on a couch and Cissy stayed in Dr. Horner's home. The next day we were on their way back to Winona.

"I guess so," I said when Cissy asked me if I thought I passed the tests.

"Were there any question you felt you couldn't answer?"

"Only one that I can remember."

"When did he say you might know the results?"

"After he sends it to wherever he sends it and they grade it, they will send the results back to Dr. Horner and then to Dr. Banks."

"I am so proud of you and happy with our friendship after all these years. You, me, Noël and Lizzy all grew up together and I feel like you are my brother and the girls, my sisters. I just love you all so much."

"You are like a sister to me too. I can always talk to you when I have a hard time with others. Your teaching and influence rounded me out. I have more confidence in myself now."

I was glad to have this time together just Cissy and me and was finally starting to feel like I was as intelligent as she thought I was. Everyone at home was so proud of me and my accomplishments. They really seemed to look up to me, the only son of a family of slaves now on his way to being a doctor of all things!

CHAPTER 50

Cissy

A couple months after Jeremiah Woodley had come to town and the Sunday after Jesse and I returned from Biloxi, Jeremiah was voted in as our new pastor even at his youthful age of thirty. The fact that he had no wife held some folks back, but he truly was the best they had heard and his background was spotless. I was smitten with him from the start but so was every other girl in town, and out of town. People road quite a ways to hear our reverend Woodley and left our church feeling truly blessed.

Everyone wanted him to come to Sunday lunch at their houses after church and of course I wanted him too as well. When I asked about it Daddy said, "I don't rightly know how he would react to our housing arrangement Cissy, maybe we should wait till he knows us better."

"How is that going to happen if the only time we see him is in church? Oh well, it doesn't really matter, he's probably heard that I was already married once and most likely the whole story about our marriage."

"Now that won't matter to a Godly man, who sees into the heart and soul of a very pretty, still young lady like yourself."

"Oh Daddy, of course you would say that."

But there was one girl at church that kept standing by him every time I saw him and that was Elizabeth Lewis, and she was also quite pretty. A blue eyed blond with curls flowing down over her shoulders and much younger than I. Oh my goodness, get over it, I kept telling myself but, how could I when every time he preached, he looked straight at me and Elizabeth sat on the opposite side of the church. But she ran to catch up with him every Sunday, even standing beside him as the people filed out and shook his hand. I thought that place was reserved for his wife if he wanted her there in the first place.

When I mentioned this on the way home, Daddy said, "Cecilia, what have I told you about prayer and waiting on the Lord? If this man is for you and God wants you to be together, there isn't one or twenty pretty girls that will stand in His way. If he marries another, then only God knows he was not right for you. If you had done that the first time, it would have saved you a lot of grief. Now you just pray and wait; I will bet he is not in that big a hurry as she is anyway."

"Oh Daddy, you make it sound so easy."

"It is easy Cissy, when you let the Lord direct your steps and trust Him. One of the hardest things of all for Christians is waiting on the Lord to answer our prayers. In a Christian's life our prayers are always answered, either yes, no, or yes but wait. If He says no, it's because he sees our life ahead of us and wants what's best for us and just because we want something so bad, doesn't mean it's going to work out well. You say you loved Jeff?"

"I know Daddy, don't even talk about that."

"Cissy, you didn't ask God about it; you led the way, not Him. Jeff was what we call a devil in angel's disguise."

"Do you think that about Jeremiah?"

"How would I know?"

"I too, thought Jeff was a nice enough young man, but we didn't know for sure about all the problems in that family. But God knew, and He allowed you to make a mistake. He is not above correcting His children and He showed you what happens when we don't let Him lead us in the right direction. Hopefully, you will do the right thing this time even if it does break your heart. Later in life you will see why He chose a different mate for you."

Next Sunday at church I was sitting in my usual pew thinking and listening so intently. Jeremiah really was a good preacher, and you could see that everyone was concentrating on his message. He was one of the few preachers that you could still remember his sermon a month later. Just something about him and his delivery showed he truly was gifted.

When we filed out of church Mommy and Daddy shook Jeremiah's hand and said a few words. When I shook his hand, he held my hand a little longer than usual and said, "I missed you the Sunday before last, hope you weren't ill?"

"No, I said, I was on a trip to Biloxi."

"Well, aren't you the one?"

"A business trip, I am afraid, not pleasure."

"I hope to see you all at the up-and-coming barn dance."

"Oh my, is it that time again already? Well sure, we are usually there. That's the most exciting thing that ever happens here in Winona, except for when we get a new preacher such as yourself."

"Well thank you Cecilia, that's very nice of you to put it that way."

"Well, you are exciting, that is I mean, your sermons are exciting."

"I do try to be prepared each Sunday."

"You are doing a wonderful job Reverend Woodley."

"Well for heaven's sake, call me Jeremiah, Cecilia."

"Well alright, outside of church, I will. Until the dance then, good day Jeremiah."

"Save me a dance or two?"

"But of course."

Mommy and Daddy were waiting outside for me with smiles on their faces. I was pretty well shaken, and they could tell. "Why does he get me all flustered?" They winked at each other. Oh, to have a love like Mommy and Daddy have! They were truly a match made in Heaven, as Daddy would say.

CHAPTER 51

Vivian

There was not much talk anymore about our place on the hill. Don't know if people lost interest or that they cared so much for Morgan now that they knew him to be a good doctor and a good man. Besides, he saved so many lives and delivered so many babies while most of them never paid him a dime. Oh, a jar of this and that, a chicken, or a ham. But he didn't care, he loved helping people and they knew it; it definitely was his calling. He stood up for what was right, and they would stand up for him because they knew he cared about them.

Jesse busied himself with his egg business. He really knew what he was doing when he built that henhouse. Everyone had fresh eggs each day. On Sunday, we took them to church, and everyone knew our eggs were freshest which meant he sold 20 dozen every Sunday. Even if he never became a doctor, he would do well with this and besides, he loved it but I did hope we heard soon about his test.

Esther grew the most gorgeous flowers in her garden, and she had a talent for arranging them so beautifully. She always made our alter arrangement for Sunday service and people bought her flowers to take home for their tables.

The ones that could, worked at doing something every waking minute of the day. Ham still made furniture and never had a spare minute to waste as people were always giving him an order for something. Big John did really well with his tobacco too and it brought a good price at auction time. Our old folks shelled the pecans we sold at church and made good money on them too. The pecans were good for all kinds of things like pies, cakes and fudge. Everyone knew that they would get their money and have things they would never have had otherwise.

Morgan always said, harvest everything you can and make something with it because you never know when the hard times will come, drought or floods or sickness, so when you have a good crop use it to the fullest and that we did. We had a pantry full of canned good for all of us to last two or three years.

We hadn't heard from Martin Catron for a while; maybe he'd settled down with that girl he brought home. I don't think he ever had a garden, just rented his land out for others to use and we never saw him at church after his family all died. We prayed for him and hoped that he would find his way.

The barn dance was next Saturday, and our family always went and so did our slaves. We needed two wagons now as our family had grown so. The women were fussing over their hair and what to wear as women always do.

Cissy decided to wear a white dress with eyelet trim and blue ribbon woven in and out through the trim on the skirt. She looked stunning and her beauty was breathtaking. As usual every eye was on her, but Elizabeth Lewis was not intimidated in the slightest by her popularity. After we arrived all the slaves went out back to their own gathering and it gave them a chance to be with their friends that they hadn't seen in a long time. This time meant a lot to them, and they had probably had a better time than we did laughing and dancing about.

CHAPTER 52

Cissy

Elizabeth was following the reverend around like before. Everywhere he moved she was right behind him. If he had stopped short, she would have run right up his back, she was that close. When the music started, he danced a square dance with her and then came over to where we sat. Again, she was right beside him while he waited for me to come back from dancing. But the reverend acted like he didn't know she was there; he came up to me and said how glad he was to see that I did come.

He asked if he might have the next dance and after I said all right, Elizabeth looked like she had swallowed a frog. She just stood there a while by herself after he took my hand and led me to where the dance was supposed to start. I said, "I hope we haven't made her mad."

"That's ok, I didn't come with her or anyone else."

"Well, she makes it look like you two are an item."

"Well, she's wrong on that account. I have had these situations before and they are hard to deal with, but I am not courting her or anyone else right now."

We danced several dances together and being a preacher he made sure we only danced the square dance which was nothing more than clasping hands as far as bodily contact was concerned. But he stayed close to me and my family for a good while and Elizabeth looked like she could claw my eyes out. She just stayed there and watched us like she was waiting to rush at him as soon as he moved away. Daddy said, "She really means business."

She made a beeline for him when he finally moved on to talk to other church members. It was kind of funny and I could tell it made him uncomfortable. But when they called for the last dance, he excused himself from her and came over and asked me to dance again. I accepted of course and she sat there alone almost in tears. Jeremiah asked me if I had a steady friend and I told him no. I also told him I was a widow and he said he knew that already.

"How long were you married?"

"Only a couple years. It was not a happy marriage; I am sorry to say."

"I know you are the teacher here. I have heard nothing but good things about you and how much the children love you."

"And I love them as well."

"I haven't ventured out as far as your place on the hill. I have heard a lot about it though."

"Well do visit us sometime, but let us know so we can be sure and be there when you decide."

"Alright, and I'll be seeing you in church?"

"Why yes of course you will."

Then we parted and got ready for the long trip home with everyone singing all the way there. Everyone had such a great evening.

Next Sunday when the church service was over, I went to get my wrap from the coat rack and there was a note pinned to my shawl. I waited till I got in the wagon and halfway home before I read it. It said, 'Leave Reverend Woodley alone.'

I showed it to Mommy and she said, "We'll discuss this when we get home." I thought, the nerve of her!

Over prayers that night in our group, I mentioned having a problem, but didn't say what it was and I asked everyone to pray for me in handling this situation. Daddy said, "Leave it in God's hands. She's the one with the problem, not you. God and the reverend will work it out without you having to do one thing. So, sleep tonight my lovely daughter, in whom I am well pleased."

CHAPTER 53

Vivian

Winter was upon us again and Morgan had become ill with influenza and was in bed for over two weeks. It was the first time he had been truly ill for as long as I could remember. I was so worried about him but didn't let on about it and besides there was plenty of work to do around the farm to keep my mind off things.

Jesse went to the clinic and helped a few patients, only because they knew he was Morgan's assistant and had seen him work alongside him on many serious cases. And believe me when you are in hard labor, a woman crying out for help gladly allowed Jesse to deliver her child. To Jesse, it seemed much easier than helping deliver farm animals, which he had been accustomed to for years anyway.

It took Morgan a while to get his strength back, but he was slowly on the mend. Him being out of commission really showed the town just how much they needed him. Even though they would not dare admit it, Jesse had stepped in and done a tremendous job for Morgan while he was out sick. Morgan trusted Jesse and knew without a doubt, Jesse could handle it. If Morgan thought the people would totally accept Jesse, he would retire and leave it all to Jesse, but he knew that wasn't going to happen at least not in his lifetime. Jesse sure could be a good doctor for his own people, right this very day.

The next Sunday after church Jeremiah asked Morgan and I if he could visit our home during the week. Morgan told him which days would be best for him, but Jeremiah wanted to know if Cissy would be there as well. With her busy teaching schedule, Friday was the day they settled on. Morgan told him if he was called out on a case, Cissy and I could entertain him and show him around.

Cissy was beside herself. "Are we going to have to hide everybody?"

"Why no! he is visiting you Cissy and probably will be oblivious to everything else going on around him. We will ask him to lunch and let him taste some of the best food he will ever have."

"I wonder if he will bring his sister Sadie too?" asked Cissy.

When Jeremiah came riding up on his horse, he looked grand and my heart was doing double time. It was around eleven and Morgan showed him around the place even taking him down to Jesse's henhouse. Morgan showed him the homes we were building for our slaves. Then they rode from one end of the property to the other. With Morgan's illness and still not being quite up to very much activity, they came on back within about forty-five minutes.

You could smell the food from out in the yard and Jeremiah remarked about how good it smelled. Morgan said, "Well I'm glad you're hungry cause these women up here do a fine job, and they are also the cause of us not having a slim one in the bunch." Even Morgan who had lost weight during his illness, had gained nearly all of it back now.

When it was time to eat all the slaves came in from the fields and crowded around the big table in the kitchen. Jeremiah was as surprised as he could be and the look on his face was priceless, but he said not a word. He was not asked to say the blessing as Morgan always did that and the grace Morgan said was not the usual, but more personal and truly from the heart.

I sat Jeremiah right across from Cissy so that they could look at one another without everyone noticing. If you are sitting right beside someone, you have to turn your head back and forth to talk to that person and it's more obvious to everyone else what's happening. Then the ladies brought the food out and started with Jeremiah, passing it around the table. Morgan explained, "Now reverend, we do this every day at lunch, that's when everyone's the hungriest. And our supper meal is served the same way but with a lighter fare. The workers will rest or sleep if they like for an hour and a half and then we go back out to our jobs till around four-thirty.   In the summertime our working hours are a might longer, but we still rest for a long period at mid-day; it helps digestion."

"You have a fine place here Dr. Banks." And while the ladies were still around the table, complemented them as well for their grand meal.

CHAPTER 54

Dr. Banks

After lunch Jeremiah and I in the front sitting room by the fire and talked about the arrangement here in our house. Jeremiah admitted he had heard stories about our treatment of slaves.

"We really don't consider them slaves and never have. I told them I merely bought their freedom." I explained it all to Jeremiah, especially how I am against owning another person and all being the same in God's eyes. "Yes, I did buy them as that was the only way I could get them, but once they were up here on this place, their chains were removed and told them to consider themselves free, at least up here on my place. Also, that no one would ever beat them for any reason. I have never had the first problem with them. They are paid and have their own garden and soon will have their own homes."

"What do they do with the money?"

"Ten percent that they save each month tithing is in the bank under my name, simply because they would not let a slave have an account and it's for their future church because they have no church. The rest they save and spend on what they want or need. These people will one day have something and a future including their own home, church, land to farm, etc. I have made sure of that. It will not be taken away from them as long as I live and my daughter will see to it after that."

"Doesn't the town give you a hard time about all this since it is against the law?"

"Now reverend, I truly don't want the town's people to know what goes on up here. They would make it hard for them and probably try to burn our house down since they already burned Jesse's henhouse down a few years back. They can't accept the fact that everyone doesn't feel the same as they do about slavery, and they get real nasty if you don't do as they say. So, it's very important that they be kept in the dark about what goes on up here. We have a large home with rooms for everyone and we are happy, and they are truly happy, just ask them. Now eventually they all will have their own homes if they like and that is what we are in the process of doing now and for our safety please do not reveal our actions up here."

Then the surprise of the day was when he asked if he could come again, and visit Cissy. "Well, that's a matter for her to decide, so why don't you ask her?"

CHAPTER 55

Jeremiah

So, the two of us walked around the outside of the house for a few minutes, but it was too cold. We came back in to go to the sitting room to get warm by the fire and everyone scattered to give us some room to ourselves. We talked about her name and the fact that I had never heard anyone call her anything but Cissy.

She asked about my relationship with Elizabeth Lewis. I told her first of all there was no relationship. Second that I had told Miss. Lewis that just because I was single didn't mean I was seeking a wife, so not to act like I belonged to her. But Cissy said, "Apparently she doesn't take no for an answer " and then told me about the note she had gotten from Miss. Lewis. Then she said, "Anyway, with demanding jobs like we both have we couldn't begin to have time for marriage. I made a terrible mistake the first time, that and being too young. Now I'm quite shy about taking that step again, for fear of failure the second time."

"When you know you have found the right one you won't be so shy. You were awfully young, Cissy."

"Yes, I think seventeen is way too young for marriage, even if many do marry at that age, you're taking a big risk. And now I think I am way too old, so I'll just enjoy my children at school. I love my work."

"You have chosen a very rewarding profession Cissy and since we are both in town most of the week, can we talk there again sometime?"

"Well sure, I mean of course, I would like that."

"I want to thank you for a lovely day. I will go in and thank your parents for having me out to your home. You are truly a remarkable and loving family."

"I do hope you make it home before dark, Reverend."

"Oh please, call me Jeremiah or even Jerry; that's what my family calls me."

"Alright then, I'm glad you had a nice day, Jeremiah."

All the way home I couldn't get the beautiful Cecilia and their whole family situation out of my mind. These are good, rooted Christians, with helping their fellow man the center of their lives. Those poor slaves are truly blessed that the Banks family came along and brought them to their home. I have no doubt this family will be remembered and have stories told about their goodness, for decades to come. When I had a few minutes with one of their slaves today, I think they called him Ham, he said, "Dr. Banks calls all our problems 'Blessings,' cause God is molding us and teaching us to be better servants of God."

And then I said, "Lord, I would consider it an honor to be a part of or friend to this family and help them in any way I could, even though your help seems to be all they need."

CHAPTER 56

Dr. Banks

Finally, a letter about Jesse. He passed with a ninety on the first test and a ninety-two on the second. I couldn't wait to tell him what a tremendous effort he had made and actually made higher marks than I had on my written exams.

I ran to find Jesse who was of course down at the henhouse. While I waved the letter in the air, I called to Jesse saying, "Look what you have done, my boy!" When I showed the letter to Jesse there was the biggest smile I had ever seen on his face. "Let's go tell your Mom and Dad," We both jumped on Jesse's horse together and rode up the hill to find Ham, Violet and the others.

We didn't even make it into the house off the porch before Ham and Violet came out to see what was the matter. I said, "Now sit down before you faint, and listen to what this letter says." It says because you have been working and studying under me for such a long period of time, plus your exceptional test scores, you can begin to treat patients on your own and this signed document is proof that you have the right to practice medicine.

"Thank you, Dr. Banks, you are responsible for this, teaching and encouraging me along when you knew my heart wasn't in it. And

Cissy, with her hard work early on, giving me the starting tools for achieving something this important."

"Cissy will be so proud of you, just as I am proud of you and always knew you could do anything you set out to do and more." Ham and Violet were crying with joy.

"When we think about the life we had led before you brought us home with you compared to now, it is just too much to believe. And our quiet Jesse, who had worked hard as a slave since he was eight years old, our only son and now this. Who in the world would have ever thought such a thing could happen? Well, God and Dr. Banks!"

"Let's go into the house now and let everyone know about this remarkable event in your life and about the celebration we are going to have, marking this achievement. Then my friend, we will have a lot to talk about, you and I."

The hard thing was keeping this news from the people in town. There are many who wouldn't like it one bit and no doubt come after him saying it's against the law, their law. So, we had to be really more careful than ever, in case this news slipped out and Jesse could and did treat a few of his own but never mentioned he had a degree. He still rode in with me and helped me because the people were used to it. Of course I paid him well. Jesse didn't mind at all told me he knew he would one day be able to practice out in the open. I thought probably sooner than he imagined and then he would reap the full benefits. Right now, he was very happy with his egg farm which was doing really well. A money maker for sure but to him a rewarding hobby.

CHAPTER 55

Jeremiah

I wasn't in a hurry to marry, but Elizabeth Lewis kept pushing it until finally one day I had her sit down and explain that I had other things on my mind (mainly Cissy Catron). She was beginning to bother me and I wasn't interested in her as far as marriage was concerned. Miss Lewis responded with contempt, "It's that Cissy Catron isn't it?"

"Ms. Catron has never done anything to you so don't be getting anyone involved in this but yourself. Because you are in this problem by yourself; I never encouraged you. Now if you will allow me to do my work here, I would appreciate it."

I could tell when she left it wasn't the end of it, but at least she knows how I feel about it.

Cissy and I met for lunch in town at least twice a week and I rode out to their farm often. I so enjoyed our time together and didn't pressure her as I really did want us to know each other very well. I laughed to myself when I thought, even if she was a cruel and heartless woman, which of course she was not, I would have a hard time leaving her because of her beauty. She had every quality my heart desired, and I has the strongest urge to do anything and everything for her. I had found the woman I wanted to share my life with forever. Now if she only felt the same. I wanted to let her be the one to let him know that and I had confidence that God was working that out.

CHAPTER 55

Jesse

It took a while to build all the houses for everyone at the farm because we all worked the fields and tended the livestock, plus their own gardens and trips to town took nearly all the hours in a day. Each one wanted a little something different in the way of fixtures in their houses, like windows and trim or a porch, etc. and that took extra time and waiting on things to be shipped into them. It was a longer, more serious undertaking than most of them had thought it would be. Actually, they got a lot more done in the winter, but it was much too cold most days to stay out that long to work on it.

The Banks didn't seem to mind at all that some were still on the hill with them, they just shared that they thought everyone would enjoy their very own house to feel freer and more private. Everyone agreed that they would welcome that but when the time came and one by one they did leave, there were many tears shed. The house on the hill had meant so much to them and then they would laugh at themselves because they were only going down the hill, not even a mile. You could still see the house on the hill from their houses and Vivian said, "Come visit anytime and every day if you like."

My new house was built as a combination home and office. In this I could see patients on the first floor and live on the second. My patient area had a big waiting room with a fireplace, a treatment room, office, and kitchen which converted into an operating room if necessary. It would be plenty for me until later when I would go into town and have my own clinic like Dr. Banks.

While staying in town several days a week with Dr. Banks I had struck up a conversation with a girl who worked at the new bakery. We often shared our lunch out under a tree behind Dr. Bank's building. I told Dr. Banks, "Her brain turned his head before her looks did," and they shared a laugh out of that. It wasn't that she had no beauty, she was nice enough looking but her sense of humor and thirst for knowledge attracted me first.

"Nothing wrong about that, my man. Beauty and no brains is hard to deal with or live with. Glad to see you have taken an interest in the fairer sex. You are a good man and any woman would be glad to have you as husband even if you are a bit to serious for your own good sometimes."

I smiled and said, "Well I am definitely serious about her!" We were married a few months later.

Cissy and the Reverend weren't in a hurry to get married. They both had rewarding jobs and wanted to get to know for sure that their love was a love that would last a lifetime. The Reverend's church attendance had grown to nearly one hundred regular attendees, so many that Pa had to make a bunch more chairs for them to put in the aisles. They changed the after church good sale to Saturday and called it Market Day, open to everyone (including me with my eggs). Everything from quilts and aprons to cakes, rolls, pies and such were sold with the usual half the proceeds going to the church. This helped the church function as so many could not give a lot and having the market on Saturday brought many folks who didn't attend church. It got almost as popular as the barn dance as it was a nice way for everyone to come together and visit.

By now a whole new council was elected and instead of a Judge when necessary allowed a jury of chosen people of their town to decide if someone was guilty and what his or her sentence should be. The town still had bitterness about the memory of the last Judge so this seemed a better way. There was also a jailer and guard which seemed to be all that was needed to keep order. Other towns of our small size had been able to accomplish this and so far so good.

Two years after they met, Cissy married Reverend Woodley in a small church ceremony with his sister Sadie as her matron of honor since she had also married a local boy a year earlier. All her pupils were in attendance and loved the whole affair and clapped hands when they said, "I now pronounce you man and wife."

The love they had was so powerful, they had four children in six years and one more as the years went on. And you guessed it, now that I am Dr. Jesse Fulton, I delivered four of them, all healthy huge babies. They lived close to town, which was close to their work and Cissy took her children to school with her till they were ready to sit in class and learn.

Dr. Banks was slowing down some now and getting close to retirement. Ma and Pa were still with them, and they were all sort of growing old together. The houses were all built and each one had growing families inside.

And a church, our very own church. We prospered because we knew our help "Cometh from the Lord," who sent a man to us that put us all in an unbelievable situation. Talk about living the "Love your neighbor as yourselves" commandment, Dr. Banks and his wife and daughter did just that.

When Dr. Banks became ill, the second time in his life, he knew it was close to his time, and he summoned Pa and me to his side. "I'm not about to go today, but I am close to leaving you, my brothers. You all know how much you mean to me and don't shed tears of anything but joy when my time comes because you know I am ready to meet my Lord and Savior. My mansion is almost ready. They're just putting on the finishing touches."

"Oh, Dr. Banks."

"Remember I told you I had a surprise for you after all the homes were built and the church and barn? I want you to make my home here on the hill a retirement home for all you folks to come when you can't take care of yourselves anymore. I want Jesse to be the doctor and overseer of all the inhabitants and their care. I don't want any of you to be without care in your last years. You have all worked too hard and deserve the best accommodations life has to offer. I will leave my entire savings and the money left here by a previous owner who was mistreated and wanted her money put to good use, and all my land to make sure this happens."

"What about Mrs. Banks?"

"I have put enough aside for my wife Vivian and if she survives me, our daughter will take care of her. Please keep the grounds in good shape and the house painted and kept up. The Lord gave me a wonderful opportunity to help my fellow man to prosper and have a better life. I want all the people of this town and the state of Mississippi to know there truly was a Heaven on the Hill."

There is a sign on the main road that says, "Fulton's Egg Farm" and an arrow pointing the way to my place. I was the largest supplier of eggs in these parts and made a trip a day to town to sell them. Even the saloon would make an egg omelet for anyone who happened to get hungry while they played poker and a new bakery in town needed lots of eggs. It was a good business and my dream come true, just like Dr. Bank's dream to come here and make a difference in people's lives.

ABOUT THE AUTHOR

Shirley Romano born Shirley Noël Meade is an acclaimed singer from the 50's-70's who was raised in Roanoke, VA with her two sisters and where she resides today. Mother to three children, two of whom are still with us today, six grandchildren, eight great-grandchildren and one great-great-grandchild, Shirley, who like Noël in this story, was born on Christmas Day and has been a gift to all who know her. Her faith like many people's faith has been challenged in her eighty plus years, but God has always provided even when she could not see the way.

Made in the USA
Columbia, SC
13 December 2022